# DEAD MAN'S HAND

A Connor Westphal Mystery

**PENNY WARNER**

P.O. Box 275
Boonsboro, Maryland 21713-0275



First Edition-May 2007
ISBN 1-59133-209-5
978-1-59133-209-1

Book Design: S. A. Reilly
Cover Illustration © S. A. Reilly
Manufactured/Printed in the United States of America
2007

To Tom, Matt, Sue, Bradley, Rebecca, and Mike
My endless source of support
And Constance Pike, my brilliant and inspirational mother

## ACKNOWLEDGMENTS

Flat Skunk Gold Stars to all those who helped with the book in some way:

Linda Allen, James Andrews, John Daniel, Susan Daniel, Andrea Farrell, Lee Goldberg, Jonnie Jacobs, Jack Jason, Amy Kossow, Peggy Lucke, Marlee Matlin, Kate Miciak, Staci McLaughlin, Ann Parker, Meredith Phillips, Connie Pike, Gail Pike, Carole Price, Dave Ridfer, Vicki Stadelhofer, Mitch Stein, the family and staff at the Mother Lode Café in Jamestown, CA, and all the wonderful fans of Connor Westphal.

Thank you.

*"Legend holds that Wild Bill Hickok was shot to death during a poker game in Deadwood, South Dakota, and that the hand he held was two pair, black aces and black eights. On that most people agree. The fifth card is not known for certain."*

*- Rules of Poker*

# 1

"What's up, Casper?" I signed to my unusually distracted signal dog as we crossed Flat Skunk's Main Street, heading for the Nugget Café.

The deep drifts blanketing the Gold Country town nearly camouflaged my snow-white Siberian Husky. If it weren't for her bright blue eyes—and her snapping head—she'd have been tough to spot in the wintry landscape.

Casper had been barking like a mad dog since we'd left my newspaper office. Not that I could hear her, but her body language was clear.

"It's just a squirrel," I said aloud, signing "squirrel" by tapping together two curled fingers under my neck.

I looked in the café windows and caught a few patrons staring at me, forkfuls of Mama Cody's cooking frozen in midair.

*A deaf woman talking and signing to her dog.*

You'd think they'd be used to us by now.

Casper's head snapped again, her tail wagging like a windshield wiper at hyper speed.

"Hush, Casper!" I signed, uncrossing my gloved hands before opening the door to the Nugget.

Little-Ruth Carter, co-leader of the New Millennium Ministry, stood in the doorway next to her older sister, Big-Ruth Carter. Both were dressed in blue hooded cloaks. At about two hundred plus pounds, Little-Ruth wasn't exactly little, but next to her super-sized sister, Big-Ruth, she looked petite.

Together they led some kind of New-Age spiritual group, housed in a once-abandoned church just outside of Flat Skunk. The religion had something to do with crystals, astrology, tarot, Chinese herbs, and perhaps a few magic mushrooms. They'd asked me several times if I wanted to "know more," but I'd politely declined.

Although Flat Skunk has its share of quirky characters like the Carters, who seek religious freedom and more or less make up their own style of salvation, there were plenty of "normal" citizens in the Gold Rush community. They just didn't make the headlines like the folks on the fringe did. We had all the usual suspects in the Mother Lode: Concerned environmentalists who cared about conserving our natural Nor-Cal resources—and those who'd burn down a forest in order to "save" a tree. Patriotic people who appreciated and protected the land of the free—and those who secretly conspired to "prevent the imminent foreign invasion." Those who smoked a little weed in the privacy of their own homes—and those who wanted to share their love of getting high with school kids.

As I squeezed by them, Little-Ruth mumbled something I couldn't lip-read—probably a blessing. While they're amiable people, I wasn't in the mood to be saved right then, so I switched to Deaf-Mode, smiled and nodded politely, and headed for the nearest booth.

As soon as I sat down, Casper started in again, this time barking at something outside the ice-laced café window, her paws scratching at the glass. Must have been an irritating sound—several diners covered their ears and glared at her. With snowflakes still on her muzzle, she looked like a rabid wolf-dog instead of her sweet furry self.

"She probably sees a squirrel," I said by way of explanation to the regulars seated nearby. Kenny-Wayne Johnson, seated in the next booth with another man I didn't recognize, gave me an approving thumbs up as if Casper were a vicious attack dog. A self-described American Mutineer, akin to a modern-day survivalist, Kenny-Wayne was probably harmless—all talk and no action. He looked like a big Teddy bear in his bulky lumberjack jacket, hovering over his honey-soaked hot cakes.

Mariposa Sunflower—or whatever her name was this week—eyed me from the next booth. Decked out in thrift shop chic and accessorized with nature-crafted bling and hennaed hands, Mariposa appeared to be taking a breakfast break from her perch in the giant sequoia tree she'd been occupying part-time for the last few weeks. The college student had been campaigning to save the forests, and was using tree-sitting to garner publicity. It seemed to be working. She'd already sold her life story to Hollywood—her life being all of nineteen years. She waved, gestured something like, "Call me," and I nodded back. She'd been on my back to write a story about her cause ever since she'd arrived in Flat Skunk. I'd promised her I would, but had been putting it off, hoping for a real story to come along and fill the front page of my weekly newspaper, the *Eureka!*

Casper barked again and after hushing her, I glanced around to see who else she had annoyed. "Chief" Dakota Goldriver—at least that's the name he went by as CFO of the new Gold Strike Indian Casino—and one of his employees who looked like Bigfoot in spite of the Sharks hockey team hat, glanced over, then quickly returned to their "Protein Platters"—five-pound omelets surrounded by strips of bacon, sausage links, and saucer-sized slices of ham. Like most of the carnivores in the Mother Lode, they had embraced the low-carb diet with open mouths. Just the smell of all that greasy high-fat food was enough to make me gain five pounds. I had a feeling they'd have Mama Cody's omelets inhaled before I could even order.

Another bark from Casper pulled me from the menu. "Casper! Hush! Or I'm going to take you outside!" I tried to look serious as I scolded her.

Kenny-Wayne tossed Casper a strip of bacon, distracting my dog for a nano-second as she sucked it in like a vacuum cleaner.

"Thanks, but she shouldn't eat bacon," I said. "It's not good for her."

"Ah, a piece a bacon never hurt nobody," Kenny-Wayne said before returning to his lard-soaked breakfast.

Casper focused her attention out the window, apparently making sure the town was free of menacing squirrels and other fun-to-chase creatures. I got to the task at hand—ordering a blueberry muffin and Mama Cody's white trash mocha (strong coffee, lots of milk, and two tablespoons of chocolate syrup), from Jilda, the waitress/manicurist/massage therapist. Then I pulled out a bunch of brochures for the latest techno-gadgets for the Deaf, set the papers in front of me, and scanned them, hoping to find an attention-grabbing headline for my weekly newspaper.

I was tired of the *Mother Lode Monitor* consistently beating the *Eureka!* at newsgathering. While their staff of twenty produced headlines worthy of "Sixty Minutes," mine tended more toward *National Enquirer* without the aliens: *Yard Ornaments Stolen!...Strange Car in Neighborhood!...Cow Loose on Rattlesnake Drive!* But after fifteen minutes of intense pondering, I still hadn't "found!" anything worth a lead story.

Maybe I was having trouble because my attention was being tugged in another direction. I pulled off my knitted gloves and twisted the gold nugget ring on my finger. Ever since Dan had used the "P" word—*proposal*—I'd been generally distracted. I knew he was surprised when I'd placed the ring on my right hand instead of my left. To me it meant *perhaps*; to Dan it seemed to mean *probably*. Whatever it meant, I'd have to make a decision soon. He was losing *patience.*

Casper interrupted my thoughts again with another round of barking. What was with her? Of course, it wasn't the noise that broke the spell—I couldn't hear her, being deaf. It was the increasingly annoyed looks coming from the Nugget patrons. Although Casper, as a working signal dog, had as much right to be in the Nugget as I did, she'd soon be shown the door if she didn't knock it off.

"Godammit!" Wolf Quick, owner of the prospecting store across the street, whirled around on his counter stool where he'd been hunched over his Hangtown Fry. In spite of the mouthful and mustache, I read his lips clearly. "Shut that stupid dog up!"

Stunned at his outburst, I glared at Wolf. "She's a *dog*! That's what she does when she sees a squirrel."

Wolf ran his hand over the top of his greasy pony-tailed hair. "Well, shut her up, for God's sake, will ya? I'm trying to eat here!"

Being deaf has its advantages. All I have to do is turn away and big-mouthed bores like Wolf Quick just disappear. I stroked Casper in an attempt to calm her, but she was obsessed with something outside.

"Quiet, Casper!" I signed and said. "You're bothering everyone! Enough!" I flicked my hand out with a twist of my wrist.

Casper stopped barking and looked at me for a moment, her tongue hanging down. I looked at Wolf and he swiveled back to his breakfast. "Good girl!" I patted her, then returned to my deaf gadget brochures.

Maybe a story on the latest, state-of-the-art Sidekick or Blackberry would intrigue hearing, as well as deaf, readers. Even kids loved the new text-messaging devices, so they could "chat" during class without their teachers' knowledge or communicate with friends while grounded at home. But more importantly, these TMs had the potential to change the way deaf and hearing people communicated. No more pencil and paper, no more confusing gestures, no more interpreters, when you could just type in your message for others to read. And text messengers were a lot less cumbersome and more portable than the old TTY/TDD—Teletypewriter Device for the Deaf.

The Voice-Over device would also make a good story. This innovative gadget translated written messages into electronic speech, offering instant communication between Deaf and hearing people. And although expensive, the Video Relay, which allowed deaf people to sign to each other via a camera attached to a telephone, was gaining popularity in the Deaf Community.

Undecided, I set down the brochures, sipped my mocha, and gazed out the crystallized window, sidetracked by the sifting snow, my agitated dog, and the weight of the gold ring on my finger. In spite of Casper's barking, the town looked deadly silent outside, a wonderland of puffy meringue pillows. Too bad the peaceful scene couldn't settle my agitated stomach.

Being from San Francisco, I loved the novelty of the snow. Folks around here are used to a little snowfall now and then, living so close to the Sierra Mountains, but this year an early storm had come to the Mother Lode, only weeks after a record-breaking heat wave. It had taken the old miners, shopkeepers, and tourists by surprise. Even Mariposa had had to buy extra snow gear for her lofty living quarters.

Maybe there was a story there: "Snow Storm Seizes Sierra!" I keyed into my Sidekick, linking up to the Internet, and typed in "snowflakes." Would my readers want to know there are seven different shapes of flakes—stars, hexagonal plates, branched crystals, needles, columns, capped columns, and irregular crystals?

I didn't think so.

How about frostbite? I conjured up another headline: *Don't Get Bitten When Jack Frost is Nippin'!* Would a sidebar offering tips on how to prevent losing your fingers get me an Associated Press pickup? I jotted down some bulleted pointers:

- Cover your skin.
- Wear loose-fitting clothes.
- Drink hot cocoa.
- Hug someone.
- If your fingers turn blue, go somewhere warmer.

*Ya think?*

Scrunching my notes into a paper ball, I felt a chill as the café door opened and a figure bundled from head to toe entered. Casper started in again, barking briefly at the padded person. I shushed her, then smiled apologetically as the figure pulled off the knitted facemask with gloved hands.

I hadn't recognized India Nicholas under all that insulation. Once she unwrapped, I noticed her puffy face and swollen eyes. Her long dark hair looked like it had been caught in a tornado. She'd obviously been crying. Needless to say, she didn't return my smile.

Jilda approached the woman, holding her six-month-old baby in tow. She gave India a one-armed hug and said something I couldn't make out. I didn't want to stare at the aging Earth Mother, but I was curious. I'd never seen India upset. Like a perennial flower child of the Sixties, she seemed to live in a garden of serenity.

Of course, it could have been a cloud of pot. She and her hippie boyfriend, Zander, called themselves "Hemp Healers," but everyone knew they were more like "Ganja Growers." It was rumored that hidden somewhere in the Sierra foothills not far from their home-made shack was a small marijuana patch where Zander and India grew weed "for their own medicinal purposes." Yeah. Sure.

But people around here tend to mind their own business, including Sheriff Mercer. He left them alone, since they didn't really bother anyone. I guess he figured the two were pretty harmless after smoking so much weed. Except when they had the munchies. Then you had to watch out.

I glanced at India as inconspicuously as I could and caught a couple of words from her lips that, even in the warm café, gave me a chill.

"...Zander...so worried...didn't come... missing..."

# 2

Before I could catch more, Casper began to act up again, pulling my attention from the distraught woman. This time she was barking at the entrance to the café. I turned to find the door open and shivered again, not from the freak snowstorm or India's words.

This cold front was blowing in with Dan Smith.

I stopped twisting the ring and waved at him cheerily. He nodded, closed the door, and shook off the falling flakes. As usual, in spite of the cold, he looked hot in his rugged black leather jacket, ubiquitous jeans, and Timberline boots. Not temperature-hot. Sexy-hot. The plaid Elmer Fudd hunter's cap with earflaps only made him look more adorable.

He peeled off his gloves and stuffed them into his pocket, shook himself out of his jacket, doffed his cap, and hung everything on the antler coat rack near the door. Mama Cody, owner of the café, greeted him with, "The usual?" while Jilda, baby attached to her hip like a fashion accessory, made a beeline for my booth with a pot of hot coffee.

It was no secret Dan and I had "hooked up," as Jilda liked to say. But that didn't stop available females from vying for his attention. Even Jilda, with little Jackson in tow—thanks to a conjugal quickie with Wolf Quick while he was doing time for fraud—couldn't help but flirt with Dan. I didn't like it, but I couldn't blame her.

Casper's attention focused on the closed door, even as Dan sat down across from me in the red leatherette booth. Pulling a doggy treat from his jeans pocket, Dan offered it to Casper, then scratched her behind both ears. I was starting to feel jealous from all the attention he was giving my dog when he reached over and took my hand. The ring hand. He swirled his thumb around the gold nugget absently, his penetrating eyes on me.

Jilda interrupted to take Dan's breakfast order. "So, what's my favorite P.I. want today?" she said, flashing her thickly mascaraed eyelashes at him.

Dan pointed to himself, then turned his palms up and closed his fingers—the signs for "me" and "want." Then he shaped a triangle by joining the tips of his index fingers and thumbs.

I choked, nearly spitting out my mocha.

"What?" Dan said aloud. "I just asked for some pie." He lowered the triangle.

I pressed my lips together and shook my head.

Jilda shrugged and headed back to the counter, clueless.

Dan looked at me. I raised an eyebrow. "That isn't the sign for pie."

He slowly let go of his triangle. "What is it then?"

"Vagina."

For the first time ever, I saw Dan blush.

He laughed and shook his head at his mistake. His smile could melt snow in the Arctic. "Well, now I know another new sign. Might come in handy some day." He took my hands again.

I quickly pulled them back. "Brrr. Your hands are freezing!" I signed the concept by shaking my fists so Dan could have the sign language practice. He'd been taking classes at the community college, but he wasn't as proficient as my young office assistant Miah, Sheriff Mercer's son.

Still, he knew how to use his hands when I wanted him to.

"Sorry." He circled his fist on his chest, then rubbed his hands. "It is a bit nippley outside." He glanced at the window.

"Did you just say 'nippley'?"

He shook his head and blushed. "Nip-py," he said over-enunciating. "Nippy. I need better gloves. The cold goes right through the ones I have. You look nice and toasty, though." He gave me an appraising look.

I could feel a whoosh of heat flood my chest and face. Early menopause? Nope. Dan Smith. He still did it for me. Then what was my problem with his "P" question?

"What are you working on?" He indicated the papers and brochures on the table.

"Looking for a story. Thought I'd write something on the latest gadgets for the Deaf. Want to buy me a Video Relay System? Then we could see each other when we talk on the phone." I spun the brochure around toward him.

His eyebrows lifted. "I could think of some creative ways to use this thing."

I snatched the ad from his hands and the thoughts from his mind. "Never mind. So, you got anything I could turn into a story for the *Eureka!*?"

An ex-New York cop, Dan had taken over his brother Boone's private investigation business after Boone died. But the PI business was fairly slow in the Mother Lode. Dan mostly handled missing persons, fraud investigation, and background checks, with only an occasional homicide.

"The usual. Terrorism. Drug cartels. Bank robbery. Claim jumping. And a couple of missing iPods."

I laughed. The closest thing we had to a terrorist in the Mother Lode was Mariposa Sunflower, who threatened to live in a tree to make her point. Claim jumping? I supposed the two Ruth's New Millennium Ministry could be accused of that, having taken over an abandoned church. Like many small towns in Northern California, we had our "drug cartels"—if you could call a small marijuana patch owned by mellow Deadheads like India and Zander a cartel. Bank robbery? Maybe highway robbery—the kind that took place at the Gold Strike Indian Casino. But iPod theft? That was some serious shit.

"I wish I had your job," I said and signed. "Never a dull moment. Got anything I can use as a headline for this week's paper? Something eye-catching and controversial?"

"What about the casino. Haven't you been getting a lot of letters about that?"

It was true. The *Eureka!* was drowning in letters to the editor, all focused on the contentious gambling casino. Ever since the government had allowed Indians to build and operate their own casinos, there had been a backlash. The environmentalists were upset about losing the land they'd worked so hard to preserve. The religious groups didn't relish the idea of gambling in the area. The survivalists just claimed Indian casinos were un-American. And the Deadheads—well, they didn't write, so they probably didn't care, as long as there was still space to grow their weed.

"You mean I should respond to these letters and stir up even more trouble—"

Casper started snapping again. As she barked, her tail wagged so fast, I thought she might go flying.

"What is it, girl?" Dan said, as the rest of the diners stopped mid-bite and turned. He offered Casper another dog treat, but this time she ignored it.

Something was up. Casper never ignored food.

Wolf rose from his seat and stomped over. "What the hell is her problem? Jesus! This dog has no business being in a restaurant. It's illegal...or something..."

As if Wolf Quick ever concerned himself about the legality of things, especially since he'd spent time in jail for fraud. I got up from the booth and faced him. "I told you, Wolf. Casper is a working dog. A signal dog. She's *legally* allowed to be here."

"I don't think she's *legally* allowed to bother customers." Wolf sneered. His twisted face didn't help my lip-reading skills but I knew what he'd said.

"I'm not sure *you're* legally allowed to bother customers, either, Wolf," I retorted.

Wolf took a step closer, his face red with anger, his hands raised.

Dan moved in before Wolf could take a swing at me. "You got a problem, man?"

Wolf looked up at Dan, looked down at me, looked farther down at Casper. "No. Just shut this dog up so I can eat my meal in peace."

Mama Cody waddled out from behind the counter, wiping her hands on her stained apron. She picked up Wolf's tab with puffy, flour-dusted fingers and slammed it down next to the register, sending a cloud of white adrift like snow.

"Your meal *is* finished, Quick," she said, looking up at him as he towered over her. Although a foot shorter and wider than the muscular, prison-honed man, she had fire in her eyes—and the keys to a full stomach. If Wolf ever wanted to eat at the Nugget Café again, he'd take the hint.

He did. He threw down a bill, grabbed half a dozen toothpicks from the shot glass that held them, and yanked his flannel-lined denim jacket off the deer antler, shaking the stand. With a last glare at me, he jerked open the front door and stomped out, leaving the door standing wide open. Casper was outside like a hound on a hare.

"Casper!" Stunned at his behavior, I bolted for the exit. "Come back! Casper!"

But she'd turned a deaf ear to me. I ran outside as she chased Wolf Quick across the street, barking every step of the way.

"*CASPER*!" I screamed. My dog had turned into Cujo. She narrowly missed being hit by an SUV, but it didn't stop her from tailing Wolf. The jeweler/ex-con fairly slid into his shop, slamming the door behind him.

But Casper had already pulled up short. Head up, she was barking wildly at something just outside the shop door. Something overhead.

I looked up, searching for a squirrel or other animal that would cause such a transformation in my usually serene dog. There was nothing except the snow-dusted wooden dummy hanging over the door of Wolf Quick's Gold Prospecting Adventures.

The historical landmark had been there seemingly forever, a symbol of the past when towns in the Mother Lode were called Hangtown, Miner's End, and Dead Man's Flat—for good reason.

The wind had picked up, causing the dummy dressed like a prospector to whip around. But I didn't feel the cold, too perplexed at Casper for disobeying me. I squatted beside her and took her by the collar.

"What's wrong with you?" I said aloud and signed one handed, literally "Wrong, you, what!" "Come!" I tried to pull her back, but she refused to budge. Shaking her head out of my grasp, she began to dig in the snow.

I crooked a finger at her, the sign for "What?" then watched her burrow her muzzle in the soft flakes. "What is it, Casper?" A chill settled into my bones as I stood in the freezing snow without my jacket, wondering what had possessed my dog. When Casper finally lifted her head, her nose was covered with pink snow.

I knew what yellow snow meant, but I'd never seen pink snow.

I brushed her nose gently, then looked at my fingers.

Someone tapped my shoulder. I spun around to see Dan holding my puffy jacket. With my attention on Casper, I hadn't noticed him come up behind me.

"What's wrong?" Dan held the jacket while I slipped it on.

I showed Dan my fingertips. We both looked down at the hole Casper had dug.

The snow was growing pinker.

I looked up. The dummy hung directly overhead. It appeared the same as it always did—like an early miner swinging from a rope for claim jumping or other gold-related crime. But as I stared at it, I noticed its tattered flannel shirt was unbuttoned and draped loosely over what appeared to be a brightly colored shirt.

Tie-dyed?

Then I noticed the denim overalls had been replaced by regular jeans. And instead of boots, the dummy now sported athletic shoes. Something dripped from one of the shoes and landed on the front of my Gallaudet University T-shirt. I wiped it off.

Blood.
I gasped. My stomach lurched.
And then I puked.

# 3

"You've got to stop throwing up on crime scenes, Connor." Dan rubbed my back as I wiped blueberry dribble from my mouth.

"Sorry," I said, "but his face…it's…" I'd tried to turn away from the sight of the black and blue image but it was like watching an accident happen. When I felt my stomach rise up again, I focused on my breathing to quiet the volcano inside.

I grimaced at Dan. "Better call Sheriff Mercer."

"No need."

"Why not—"

Dan nodded toward the Nugget Café.

I followed his gaze and understood immediately what he meant. A dozen bobbing heads stared out the café windows, eyes wide, mouths open, ears attached to cell phones. I guess they'd seen me hurling and figured out the cause. Sheriff Mercer's phone was probably ringing off the hook, although with his office only a few yards down Main Street, he could just as easily lean out the window and hear the yelling. At any rate, he'd be arriving in a matter of minutes.

The curious breakfasters began streaming out of the Nugget for a closer look. Shop owners up and down Main peered out from their front steps. Even Mama Cody, who rarely leaves her grill, arrived wiping her hands on her Jackson Pollock splattered apron to see what had dragged her customers from their meat pasties and Hangtown Fry.

Nothing goes unnoticed in Flat Skunk. Not even with hearing people.

Even though I'm deaf, I can faintly hear very low sounds, like airplanes, and very high sounds, like police sirens. A shrill irritation caught my attention. It seemed to come from someone in the crowd.

The onlookers turned to the source of the sound and I followed their stares. India, her hand over her mouth, stood on the outskirts of the crowd, gazing up at the swinging corpse, screaming. When she dropped her hand, I read her lips: "Zander..."

I glanced back up at the swinging corpse. *My God. It was Zander Nicholas!*

"Someone get her away from here!" Dan shouted.

Jilda stepped up with her baby, put her free arm around the hysterical woman, and led her back to the café. I felt for India as she collapsed into Jilda. The poor woman. She and Zander had been living the hippie lifestyle out in the boonies for years. When they came to town for supplies and the occasional breakfast at the Nugget, they were always together. I wondered what India would do now, all alone in that ramshackle home, except for a bunch of dogs. Rumor was they kept over a dozen wolves as pets out there—to keep away marijuana claim-jumpers, no doubt.

I turned back to Dan. He was shouting something I couldn't make out, trying to keep the onlookers at bay until the sheriff arrived. I caught a glimpse of Wolf Quick standing in the doorway of his shop, watching the scene with little expression.

How long had he been there?

And how long had he been holding that rifle?

Instinctively I tightened my grasp on Casper.

"What are you planning to do with that?" I shouted at Wolf, indicating the rifle.

He looked at me nonplussed. "What the hell is going on out here?"

Did he really not know there was a dead man—a real one—hanging over the front door of his shop?

"You want to put that rifle down, Quick?" Dan said, taking a step toward him. In spite of Wolf's prison workouts, if they came to blows, Dan, the ex-New York cop, would win hands down.

Wolf looked at the rifle, shrugged, and leaned it against the door jam, then stepped onto the wood plank broad way.

The café patrons had inched forward, forming a tight circle around Dan, Casper, and me. But they weren't looking at us. All eyes gazed upward, on the body of Zander Nicholas above our heads.

I spotted Sheriff Mercer hustling down the street, his rapid breaths visible in the cold air. Marca Clemens, his deputy, trailed after him, carrying a small suitcase—her crime scene kit. By the time the sheriff arrived, he was huffing and puffing like a fireplace bellows. The guy either needed Pilates or an inhaler.

"Stand back!" he yelled, waving his hands. The onlookers stepped back half an inch. "Stand back!" he yelled again, this time gesturing at Deputy Clemens to handle crowd control. She set down her kit, hoisted her fifty-pound belt, and officially took over the yelling and waving.

"All right, now, what the hell is going on?" Sheriff Mercer said to Dan and me. The sheriff is easy to read, thanks to the lack of mustache and chewing tobacco. And he'd become more aware of facing me when he talked, now that he wore a hearing aid himself.

He briefly scanned the snow-covered area beneath the body looking for a clue, then returned his attention to us. "Rebecca just got half a dozen calls at dispatch and none of them made any sense. A hanging body? A live dummy? A swinging corpse? C.W., what the hell are you up to this time?"

"Nothing, Sheriff!" I snapped and nodded at my dog. "It was Casper. I thought she was barking at a squirrel, then she started digging, the snow was pink, then I looked up and..." I gestured around wildly like a confused traffic cop.

But the sheriff had already stopped listening to me. He was rubbing his forehead and gazing up at Zander Nicolas's corpse.

"What the hell...?"

By the time Dr. Arthurlene Jackson, the medical examiner, arrived twenty minutes later with her assistant, Sus Takeda, the crowd had been hustled back inside the Nugget. I could see through the window that none of them had gone back to their meals. They were all too busy chewing on the subject at hand.

While Dan took a look around at the snow-covered street, Sheriff Mercer started up one of Wolf's ladders to the roof to survey the area. "I'm guessing it's a suicide," the sheriff called down. "Most hangings are these days, unlike the Forty-Niner days. But we won't know for sure until Arthurlene does the autopsy. In the meantime, stay outta the crime scene, C.W." With that, he continued his climb, his foot slipping every other step, thanks to his icy shoes.

I held my breath until he reached the top, not sure he was going to make it. When he was out of sight, I pulled out my notebook and studied the body, clutching my pen with a death grip. I needed to put together a story for the *Eureka!* before the EMTs arrived and shooed me out of the way. But by the time they reached the site five minutes later, I still had nothing. All I could do was watch as they joined the sheriff on the roof and carefully lowered the body from its post onto a waiting gurney.

Zander was clearly dead—there would be no need for resuscitation. According to the EMTs, the mottled skin, swollen lips and tongue, bulging eyes, and damp crotch were all indicators he'd died from asphyxiation. Of course, that much I knew from watching the deaf investigator, "*Sue Thomas: F B Eye,*" on TV. I thought the sheriff was probably right about suicide until I noticed Arthurlene holding up Zander's lifeless hand. She examined it closely, like a fortuneteller reading a secret within a palm.

I inched over, not wanting to disturb her for fear she'd shoo me away too. Arthurlene and I weren't exactly friends, but we respected each other and had found a nice balance when working together—if I kept mostly out of her way, she deigned to give me the occasional crumb of information.

I sidled up closer to the body and immediately took in a mixture of pungent odors, some distinctly unpleasant. But one was familiar from my college days. Zander's clothes still reeked of the sweet scent of marijuana.

I inhaled again deeply to be sure.

"You're breathing on me," Arthurlene said, turning her head over her shoulder so I could lip-read her.

"Sorry," I said. Damn this cold air. I couldn't even keep my breathing from irritating her. "What's with the hand?"

She said nothing. I peered in closer and caught a glimpse of something shiny. In the grip of rigor mortis—or frostbite—Zander held what looked like a large gold coin in his stiff palm.

Arthurlene pried open his fingers and tried to gently lift the object out with tweezers. The coin wouldn't give. Arthurlene frowned, then tried again, this time digging under the coin with the tweezers to get a better grasp. With a tug, she dislodged the coin and held it up, then glanced back at the dead man's hand.

"Superglued," she said, her frown deepening. She returned her attention to the gilded gambling token. I could just make out the imprinted words: *Gold Strike Indian Casino*.

"It was glued to his palm?" I said, puzzled. "How odd..."

Arthurlene dropped the coin into a paper evidence bag that Sus Takeda held ready for her, then indicated for him to bag Zander's hands.

A shadow appeared and I looked up to see Sheriff Mercer lumbering down the ladder.

"Did you find anything up there?" I asked when he joined us. "Like a half-naked dummy or a note or something?"

The sheriff ignored me and turned his attention to Arthurlene. "What have you got?"

We deaf people are often ignored. Sometimes I use it to my advantage, like when I'm trying to get a story for the paper. If hearing people think you're not paying attention because you're deaf, they often say something they normally wouldn't. I've gathered more than a little information by being a fish out of water.

But most of the time being ignored is just annoying. Like now. I tried again, this time with Arthurlene. "So, Doc, what do you think that coin glued to his palm means?"

Arthurlene said something to Sheriff Mercer that I couldn't make out, but I was certain it had nothing to do with my question. She pointed to Zander's neck with a red manicured nail. There were dark bruises on the discolored skin—rope burns—a clear indication of hanging. No surprise. But Arthurlene frowned again as she pointed out some other marks on Zander's neck.

I moved so I could read her lips and caught her in mid-sentence. "...scratches, as if he were pulling at the rope..."

The sheriff lifted one of the dead man's hands, removed the bag and examined the stained, stubby nails. "You think maybe he changed his mind about killing himself?" he asked.

Arthurlene shrugged. "It happens. Depends on what we find under his nails. I also found this glued to his hand." She removed the gambling chip from the bag with tweezers. "Must have been important to him if he glued it to his hand."

The sheriff nodded and rubbed his forehead. "Shit. I'll bet the house this was no suicide."

"Why, Sheriff?" I asked, hoping he'd finally notice the invisible deaf person standing next to him.

He pulled his hand away from his forehead, leaving a red streak where he'd rubbed the skin nearly raw.

"'Cause someone else was up on that roof with him."

# 4

"How do you know?" I asked the sheriff after he dropped that little bombshell. "Two sets of footprints?"

Sheriff Mercer shook his head. "Nope. Last night's snowfall took care of finding that kind of evidence. But there was something." He paused for effect, eying me, then held up what looked like a bracelet made of pine needles, with a golden-centered white silk flower woven into it. "I don't think Zander wore this kind of girlie jewelry."

"So you think someone...dropped it up there?"

He shrugged. Since he was in a semi-talkative mood, I asked, "Anything else?"

"A half-naked dummy."

"I just asked you that!"

The sheriff ignored me. "I can understand hanging yourself, but why go to the trouble of removing the dummy, taking off the shirt, putting it on the body, gluing a coin to your palm, and then..." He left the thought unfinished.

I glanced at the ladder. "Can I take a quick look? I won't step on anything, I promise."

"Hell, no, C.W.! It's slicker than a frog's belly up there. I nearly fell on my ass a couple of times. You're staying right here where I can see you."

With that, the sheriff took a step toward Zander's ambulance, slipped on an icy patch of the street, and fell on his khaki-covered ass.

"GODdammit!" he yelled as he tried to stand up. I ran over to help him but he shook me off. "I'm fine! I'm fine! Just give me a minute."

He rolled over in the snow, trying to find purchase, but his leg slipped out from under him. I saw him wince from the pain. An EMT ran over and knelt down. While the tech examined the sheriff's ankle, the two exchanged a few words I couldn't read. The EMT waved his partner over.

"Bring a splint. I think his ankle's broken."

"GODdammit!" the sheriff cursed again.

"Hey, it's a good thing you didn't fall off the roof," I said.

He shot me an icy look.

I backed off and busied myself with my reporter's notebook, while the EMTs carted the sheriff into the waiting ambulance and took off for Mother Lode Hospital—the sheriff to hospital Emergency, the corpse to the hospital morgue.

Sheriff Mercer refused to let me accompany him to the emergency room, and Arthurlene Jackson wouldn't let me follow her to the morgue for the autopsy. I had no choice but to return to my office and perform my own bodyless autopsy in an effort to come up with something for my newspaper. At least I finally had a real story. Only problem was, I didn't think I'd ever get that last image Zander Nicholas out of my mind.

"Come on, Casper," I signed to my dog, tapping the side of my leg. We headed to my building down the street, and up the stairs to my newspaper office. The *Eureka!* is housed upstairs in an old hotel and former brothel that now sported boutiques, antique shops, and other tourist traps on the first floor. In addition to my newspaper, the second floor offered office space to Dan Smith, Private Investigations, and Jeremiah Mercer, owner of his own comic book/surf shop.

I passed Dan's office and arrived at my neighboring office to find the door standing ajar. With the memory of the dead man still fresh in my mind, I paused and peeked inside. Casper rushed in before I could stop her.

"Casper!" I commanded.

Miah, the sheriff's son and my part-time assistant/interpreter, looked up from his laptop, startled.

"Do you have to scream so loud?" he signed. Literally he'd said, "Scream! Must you? Loud!" He turned back to his hunting and pecking.

I circled my chest with a fist. "Sorry," I said. "I keep forgetting you're a hearie." It was true—I was always surprised that hearing people startled at some sounds. What was up with that? Sounds could be so loud they scared hearing people? "So did you hear the news?"

Miah shook his head as he stared at his computer screen, already deep in concentration.

"What are you working on? Something important?" Literally, *work you, what? Important?*

I walked over and peered at his screen.

An armed man in a uniform and helmet popped up, aiming his gun directly at Miah. The soldier began to shoot.

"Oh my God." I looked at Miah in disbelief. "I can't believe you're playing 'Tour of Duty'! I thought you were working on the casino story!"

"It's 'Call of Duty,' not 'Tour of Duty,'" Miah signed. He punched some keys and the soldier fell to the ground.

"Miah! Stop killing Germans! Don't you know what just happened?"

Miah suddenly jerked, as if having a seizure, then dropped the joystick. Apparently he'd been shot. Game over. Exasperated, he turned to me and signed slowly for emphasis. "Just because I can hear doesn't mean I can hear through walls, so if something happened outside this room, I'm afraid I missed it. And now I'm dead—thanks to you."

"You're not the only one," I said, moving around to my own computer and tapping the keyboard. The screensaver lit up—a view of the Sierra Nevada mountains in the spring, filled with mustard weed, buttercups, and California Poppies. I hoped the picture would keep me going through the next few months of winter.

Miah sat back. "What do you mean?" *What mean you?*

"Didn't you even hear the sirens?" *Hear siren, you?*

"You know Dad turns on those lights and sirens every chance he gets. He's like a kid with a toy car. He used them twice yesterday. One was for that 'emergency' call about dope smokers in the town gazebo, and the other for a tourist who thought Sluice was an escaped lunatic."

Sluice Jackson, Flat Skunk's mascot, was a nearly century-old prospector who may have been short a couple nuggets, but he was no lunatic. He just looked like one. Although he'd recently inherited a large sum of money from a deceased relative, he still maintained his old lifestyle, working at the mortuary, drinking at the gazebo, and selling beaded earrings that hung on his weathered cap.

As for the dope smokers, they were routine in these parts. Around here many folks still believe in their right to bear arms, spit in public, and smoke fatties whenever they feel the urge. Live and let live, unless you're in my business.

"Well, you're missing a big story," I signed, then keyed in my password—Casper—and opened up a file. The blank screen mocked me as it always did when I first confronted it.

"What's up?" Miah signed, twisting his wrists and flipping his palms up, middle fingers slightly extended. "Someone at the Nugget finally keel over after eating all that lard?"

This week Miah had become a vegetarian. He'd decided not to eat anything that had a face or tasted good. Last week he was on Atkins, even though there wasn't an ounce of fat on him. The week before it was Krispy Kremes and Jamba Juice.

"No. Zander Nicholas...died. Your dad thought it was a suicide at first, but now he thinks it may be a homicide."

"Zander? That old hippie guy?"

"He's not that old—forty or so. Maybe fifty. I don't know. But yeah, that's the one."

"Yeah, I see him in town once in a while. Lives with that hippie woman out in the boonies. They always seem like they've horked a few too many 'brownies.'"

I laughed. "You ever had any of those 'brownies'?"

"Nah. I'm not into that crap. Kills your brain cells. Is that how he died? Brain damage?"

"Not exactly. You know the Hanging Dummy that swings over Wolf's shop?"

Miah nodded.

"It was replaced." I gave him a long look.

"With what?"

Apparently I was going to have to fingerspell it out for him.

"Z-A-N-D-E-R."

He grimaced as the letters took shape from. "No shit! Whoa! How? What happened?"

I shrugged. "Your dad isn't exactly sure. Like I said, it looked like a suicide, but he checked the roof, found something—he wouldn't tell me what—and figured Zander wasn't alone up there."

"You mean, someone *hung* him?" Miah held an imaginary rope around his neck, then stuck out his tongue.

I nodded.

"Who?" His index finger circled his mouth.

I shrugged one shoulder. "Whoever it was went to a lot of trouble to make a statement. It must not have been easy, getting him up there, replacing the dummy, and then hanging him like that. Especially in the dark. And in the snow."

Miah looked lost in thought.

"By the way, your dad's in Emergency. He slipped—"

Miah stood up. "Off the roof! Why didn't you tell me?"

I waved my hand down. "No, not off the roof. On the street. He's all right. Probably bruised his ankle or something."

Miah slowly sat back down, grinning. "You're kidding. He slipped on the street? Maybe he'll retire on disability now."

"Not your dad. He'll be a cop to his dying day."

I turned back to my keyboard and typed the first of many less-than-compelling headlines, finally settling on "Dead Man Hanging." It was a work in progress.

Miah waved in my peripheral vision to get my attention.

"What?" I flipped my hand up

"Do you think it's drug related?"

"Your dad's fall?" I teased. "Oh, you mean Zander? Don't know. Could be. But who'd want to off someone who minds his own business and doesn't bother anyone? And if the killer is a druggie who gets pot from them, then he's just killed off the source of his smoking pleasure."

I stared at my headline. As eager as I was to write the story, nothing further would come. Maybe that was because I didn't have anything other than a headline.

I looked over the latest "Sheriff's Reports" that Rebecca Matthews, the sheriff's eighty-something dispatcher, had emailed me. Maybe I could find a story there, until I learned more about Zander's death.

> *"6:21 pm – Fiddletown. Someone at a motel on South Jackass Road called 911 because the coffee maker in the room was not working properly."*
>
> *"7:23 pm – Soulsbyville. The driver of a black SUV pulled out in front of the driver of another SUV and yelled profanities."*
>
> *"10:39 pm – Railroad Flat. A report of a large brown-and-white cow in the back yard of a home on Jail Street."*
>
> *"11:42 pm – Drytown. A woman on Flat Tire Road said when she was burning debris in her backyard, she accidentally threw in a box of ammunition and some of the bullets went off."*

Who'd believe all this? I thought as I typed in the details. Except there was no way I could make this stuff up.

Oh well, it was something to do while I waited for the report from Arthurlene Jackson or Sheriff Mercer. But afterward, I promised myself, I'd do some real investigative reporting. Something about the body was bothering me—besides the sheer weirdness of it.

Why would Zander glue a gambling token to his palm?

I swung by the Nugget Cafe, Casper at my side, to see if India, Zander's common-law wife, was still there. According to Jilda, India had been gone at least half an hour. She didn't have much more to offer in the way of information, only that the new widow had returned home to feed her animals.

Odd, I thought. Zander, her long-time partner, is dead under mysterious circumstances and she's thinking about her pets? I patted Casper. If something happened to Dan, would my first thought be that I had to feed my dog? Maybe.

Casper and I hopped in my Chevy and headed down the long and winding road that supposedly led to Zander's place. I'd never been there before, but everyone in town seemed to know where the couple lived—about five miles out Poker Flat Road.

The area had once been filled with active gold-spewing mines, but nothing much was left of the once rich deposits aside from abandoned caves, polluted rivers, piles of tailing, and arsenic deposits, thanks to hydraulic mining. According to local gossip, Zander and India moved out here twenty years ago and had squatted on government-owned land. They'd immediately begun resoiling, reseeding, and replanting the stripped and depleted area. That's probably why the local officials hadn't kicked them off.

The landscape changed dramatically when I hit the last couple of miles. Instead of barren snow-covered land, groves of orange and olive trees flourished over the rolling hills. I wondered how far back Zander's gardens grew. I'd seen him and India on most Saturdays at the Farmer's Market, selling their produce. Apparently that's how they made enough money to live. Unless they also dealt in some minor marijuana sales. As I scanned the acreage, I wondered how they managed to cultivate all the fruits of their labor. It was way too much for just two people.

I knew I was getting close when the hand-crafted and misspelled. warning signs began to appear along the potholed country road: *Keep Out!...Danger!...No Tresspassing!...Bewear of Vichious Dogs!* One was even written in Spanish: *Pare! Peligro!* I knew the second word meant "Danger!"

Then suddenly the craftsman's cottage—actually more of a prospector's shack—appeared out of nowhere, nestled in a blanket of snow. A barbed wire fence encircled the tiny cottage, the only entrance a chain-locked gate. I didn't blame them for discouraging attempts to invade their privacy and protect themselves way out here. No one would hear me if I screamed in this deserted spot. Certainly not me.

I parked the car, cracked the window, and stepped out, leaving Casper inside.

In fact, no one would even find me if something happened, I thought as I closed the car door. The hairs on the back of my neck prickled.

Before I could get back in the car and forget the whole thing, the front door of the cottage burst open.

I caught my breath and froze, half expecting to see a dozen vicious attack dogs snarling in the doorway.

What I didn't expect to see was the business end of a double-barreled shotgun.

Aimed at me.

# 5

I stepped back, hands up, heart in my throat.

"Don't shoot! It's me...uh, Connor Westphal." Scared shitless, I almost forgot my own name.

The barrel of the shotgun pushed the door open another inch. Four snarling, snapping dogs squeezed through the space and leapt out on the rickety porch, teeth bared and drool falling from their muzzles. They looked like wolves; in fact, they looked a lot like Casper, my Siberian Husky.

But with bigger eyes and sharper teeth.

I felt like Red Riding Hood.

A figure stepped out from behind the fur and shadows.

"India?" I managed to say. I only hoped my voice was loud enough for her to hear over the barking wolf-dogs.

She frowned as if trying to place me. Her long gypsy skirt and heavy cable sweater appeared disheveled. Her puffy face was streaked with tear tracks and the lids of her red-rimmed eyes were swollen, making her look older than her years. She'd twisted her long hair up into a large messy knot, the ends sticking out like prickly weeds.

She looked kind of crazed.

I cleared my heart out of my throat and babbled on. "Yeah...my name is Connor Westphal...I publish the *Eureka!* newspaper...in Flat Skunk..." I pointed to myself, then down the road, as if she could see my building from her porch. Lowering my hands, I hoped she'd follow suit and lower the gun.

She didn't.

Instead, she said something I couldn't lip-read at that distance. I took a step forward and pointed to my ear. "What? Sorry, I can't hear you. I'm deaf."

I might not have been able to read her lips, but her facial expression was clear—a look of confusion offset by pity as she realized I had a disability. It was a reaction I often got when hearing people found out I was deaf.

I gestured again for her to lower the gun and stepped forward, taking advantage of her "poor deaf woman—she's harmless" assumption. India let the barrel of the shotgun drop as she stepped onto the porch, her dogs still barking frantically beside her. Her face was partially blocked by hanging rope crafts, flowerpot holders, windsocks, and geometrical tableaus that swayed gently from the eaves of the cottage.

She shouted a command at the dogs that I couldn't quite make out, something like "pa-lay" or "ba-lay." Tough to tell "P" and "B" apart on the lips. Whatever she said, it worked. The dogs grew tranquil, hung their heads, and slunk back through the front door, hindquarters wagging in shame. I glanced over at Casper to see how she was dealing with the canine threats. Her paws were on the car windowsill, ears perked up, tongue hanging out. Her dog language was clear: "Thank God I'm in here."

I turned back to India, catching her in mid-sentence. Apparently she'd forgotten I was deaf and had started talking without getting my attention first. Happened all the time.

"What?" I moved closer so her face wasn't obscured by the hanging ropes. I caught the sweet smell of marijuana wafting from inside the house.

"I *said*, what are you do-ing here?" She over-enunicated, to the point of almost obsuring her speech. "This is private pro-per-ty."

"Yes...I was working on an obituary for Zander—for my newspaper—and I wanted to ask you a few questions." I paused, then threw in, "I'm sorry for your loss."

She frowned again, squinting her eyes as if she were trying to read the real reason behind my visit. Not a very friendly woman, I thought. When she didn't say anything I changed the subject, hoping to gain her trust.

"Your dogs are really well trained. Did you train them yourself?"

She shook her head. "Zander did. He has—had—a gift."

"They look like wolves."

"They're not. At least, not pure. They're mixes. And they're legal."

*Legal?* Odd thing to say. "Well, they're beautiful."

"Zander loved them..." Tears welled at the mention of his name. Pulling a tissue from a deep pocket in her long tie-dyed skirt, she pressed it to her face.

I talked on, hoping to distract her from a full-on crying jag. "You must love dogs. Being deaf, I trained my dog Casper to respond to sign language. She knows all kinds of signs, like...uh, go home..."

I knew I was rambling, but she made me nervous standing there with the shotgun dangling from one arm, her dogs vigilantly peeking out from behind her.

"Anyway, the reason I'm here...I wanted to write an accurate story about Zander since he was somewhat of a mystery to many folks around here. I wondered if you might have a few special things to tell me about him."

She shook her head. "He wouldn't want that. He was a very private man."

I glanced at the barbed wire and remembered the warning signs I'd passed.

"Okay, well..." I tried another tack. "Is there anything I can do for you—?"

"I'll be fine," she snapped, not letting me finish.

I scanned the snowy acres surrounding the shack. "Aren't you nervous being alone way out here?"

"I got my dogs. And this." She held up the gun. "Zander made this place good and safe. He had to, on account of...well, you never know these days. Lotsa crazy people out there."

I nodded. "It's a beautiful...area." I couldn't say much for the living quarters, but the land was heavily planted and obviously well cared for. Again I wondered where all the help was.

"Do you grow all your own foods?"

She nodded.

"Got a garden out back."

"And those...rope things?" I didn't know what to call the woven pieces that hung from the front eaves. Art? Crafts? White trash sculptures? "You made those?"

"I make 'em and sell 'em," she said, reaching for a windsock. "Make my own rope, too."

As she let down her guard a little, I took the opportunity to move closer and pretended to admire a tie-dyed wall hanging the size of a couch throw. The thin rope felt rough and had a faintly familiar earthy smell to it.

"It's hemp," she said, and added, as if anticipating my question, "And it's legal, too."

Why so defensive? I wondered. The unlawful use of craft materials—a felony? Wouldn't have occurred to me.

"They're...very nice. How much for this?" I pointed to the wall hanging that might look nice on my living room wall if I ever went blind.

"Twenty bucks. Cash."

I nodded, said, "Be right back," and headed for the car to get my wallet from my backpack. I wouldn't be caught dead with the hippie artifact hanging in my diner-home, but Beau Pascal, who ran the Mark Twain Slept Here Bed and Breakfast in town, would probably love it.

I paid India, thanked her, and returned to the car, frustrated at not being invited inside or getting the information I had come for. I was curious about what all she had in that house, but it was clear she wasn't hosting any home tours or giving interviews today. If I wanted to find out anything more about Zander Nicholas—how he lived, what he was like, and possibly why he died—I'd have to come up with a better plan of attack.

I patted Casper, then backed down the narrow lane to a pullout area a few yards away, turned the Chevy around and headed down the icy dirt road. In my rearview mirror I caught a glimpse of India watching me, gun and dogs at her side, until I was out of sight.

Weird woman. But then you'd have to be eccentric to live such an isolated existence, I thought.

Apparently I was thinking too much, because when a deer bolted from the trees and ran across the road, I nearly hit him. I slammed on the brakes, causing the Chevy to skid off the icy lane and into a ditch before coming to an abrupt stop.

When my heartbeat slowed and I could breathe again, I checked on Casper, who had slid to the floor during the sudden stop. She barked once, then jumped back into her shotgun seat, trembling.

"Why didn't you have your seatbelt on?" I scolded her gently and gave her a hug and a once over to see if she'd been hurt. No signs of blood or broken bones or bruised—or pink—noses. But Casper was panting and drooling—a sign of her instinctual fear.

"Sorry, Casper. Mommy wasn't paying enough attention to this narrow, windy, icy, stupid road." I checked my surroundings and guessed, by the lean of the car, I was in some kind of ditch. Shifting into drive, I stepped on the gas and gunned the engine.

I felt the vibration of the car, but nothing happened.

I tried again.

Nothing, except a shaking steering wheel and a slushy spray of muddy snow spewing forth by spinning tires. We were going nowhere, fast.

"Damn-stupid-idiotic-asinine country road." I pulled out my Sidekick, flipped it open, and waited for the signal.

No signal.

I increased the cursing. "Shit-goddamn-it-to-hell-and-back." Casper looked at me. "Sorry," I said, feeling guilty. My poor dog didn't need to hear that kind of talk.

I opened the car door and stepped into the snow to survey my surroundings. Zander Nicholas' cultivated acres were behind me. Snow-frosted pines lined one side of the road, forming the edge of a dense forest. On the other side of the road stretched miles of white flat land that had been devastated by the prospecting Forty-Niners.

I'd never get wireless reception way out here

I pulled my jacket tight, let Casper out, and started making my way in the dead land. Stepping carefully through the snow, a challenge in itself, I prayed I wouldn't stumble on any hidden potholes or fall into an abandoned mine shaft. Every few steps, I checked my Sidekick in search of a signal.

When Casper and I had hiked in about five minutes, I tried my Sidekick again.

A signal!

"Yippee!" I called to Casper. She did what I thought was a "Yippee Dance," but it turned out to be her Pee-Pee Dance. She squatted near a lacy tumbleweed. Steam rose as the snow melted.

With chilled thumbs I keyed in Dan's number, then typed in the word, "Stuck!" then adding a rhyming curse. Seconds later I read the incoming message. "What's up?"

After I explained my predicament, Dan said he'd be there in twenty minutes to give my Chevy a shove with his pickup. I turned off the Sidekick and was about to head back to the warmth of the car when a cold flurry of wind lifted my hair. With it came a familiar aroma. I sniffed a couple of times. It was the third time that day I'd inhaled that sweet scent. Curious, I headed in the direction of the smell, creating snow prints with my pink Uggs, until I came to an eight-foot stone fence.

The rock wall, made mostly from ancient volcanic ash, had obviously been stacked and cemented by a novice fence builder. It looked as if the whole thing could tumble down like a row of dominoes in the next minor earthquake. I gave the wall a push to test my theory but it held firm.

Odd, I thought. A rock wall in the middle of nowhere. Curiouser and curiouser, as Alice would say. And with all the snow, I really felt as if I were in Wonderland. I grabbed hold of a jutting rock on the wall and stepped up on another, feeling like one of those pseudo rock-climbers at the gym. After a couple of missteps and one broken nail, I was able to peer over the top of the wall. I held my breath, expecting to see the remnants of an old insane asylum or a nuclear weapons facility or a secret coven of Wiccans.

Nothing so mysterious or romantic—it was an ordinary greenhouse. A hothouse, in fact. For warm-blooded plants. In the middle of the snow-covered tundra.

Another garden, growing under artificial lights? Maybe. Except for one thing. The fiberglass roof was covered with ivy. Snow-covered ivy.

Ivy? In the gold country? I reached over and tried to pluck off a leaf. It wouldn't give. I tugged harder. The whole vine came with it.

Artificial.

I leaned over a crack in the dirt-encrusted roof and peered inside. Through the hole, I could see rows of lights, and just make out the feathery plants. They looked like my favorite vegetable—California artichokes. Only these weren't chokes. And this was no ordinary garden.

This was a marijuana farm.

Big time.

# 6

Deaf people don't have Super Nostrils just because they can't hear. But we do tune into our other senses more to compensate for the hearing loss. And I knew a pot farm when I smelled one. You can't go to college—even Gallaudet University for the Deaf—without experiencing that unique aroma.

Even if you don't inhale.

I stared out at the walled expanse of moneymaking plants and tapped the fiberglass roof. It was surprisingly cool to the touch, apparently well insulated from the indoor heaters and grow lights. This operation had to cost something. It couldn't be cheap keeping marijuana plants warm and toasty in this weather. Someone had gone to a lot of trouble to make sure the crop was protected—and well hidden—year round.

Zander Nicholas? India? It was certainly close enough to their homestead.

Or was it run by someone else?

Before I could come up with a longer list of suspects, I felt a stinging blow from behind. Right on my ass.

My right butt cheek stung. I whipped around to face my attacker, brushing the remnants of the weapon from my rear end.

"Throwing snowballs?" I said to Dan. He stood below me, ready with another missile. I jumped down from the rock wall. "How childish."

"Childish?" He grinned evilly and threw the second snowball, narrowly missing my chest. It struck the stone wall behind me and crumbled into flakes. "Talk about childish. Climbing fences where you don't belong? Driving in the snow without chains? Snooping around in the middle of nowhere? I'd call that childish."

"Yeah, well, you missed me!" I picked up a clump of snow and cupped it into a tight ball. "So how did you find me?"

He did the same. "Followed your snow prints."

Before he finished making his snowball, I threw mine and got him in the shoulder. He tried to get me back but I swerved, then slipped and fell to the snowy ground. Casper added to my humiliation by licking my face.

Dan laughed. "You look like 'Smilla Falling in Snow'."

"You're mixing up your book titles," I said, awkwardly pushing myself to my feet and covertly grabbing another handful of snowy powder. I raised my arm, feeling like the Pillsbury Doughboy in my layers of clothing and puffy jacket, and threw the snowball. It would have been a direct hit if Dan hadn't ducked. I bent down, collected another handful, and swung my arm back.

"Get down!" He grabbed my arm and pulled me to the ground, covering me with his body.

"What? You want snow sex—"

He hushed me, his eyes wide, his muscles locked tight.

"What?" I mouthed.

"You didn't hear that?" he signed, pointing to his ear and shaking his head. I gave him a blank look. He stuck out his index finger and thumb. "Gunshot." Reaching into his jacket, he pulled out his gun.

I blinked. Holy shit. These pot growers took their work seriously. Suddenly I felt as vulnerable as a revenuer at an Appalachian still. And me without a snowball.

There had already been one death in the past twenty-four hours. Was some crazed killer running around shooting people at random? Or was this about the pot farm? I huddled closer to Dan and his gun.

A muffled sound ripped through the quiet. This time I heard it. "Where is it coming from?" I signed, essentially

"Where-from?" Although I could hear the report, I couldn't locate the source.

"Don't know," he signed, turning his hand away from his forehead. "There's an echo here. But that one was closer." Literally, "Echo. Close." Then, "You-and-me, go, car."

I nodded.

Dan took off, running like a hunched bear, pulling me along by my hand. Casper sprinted behind us as we scurried across the powdery snow. It wasn't easy in my Uggs. I only hoped I didn't slip and fall again like some dumb girl in one of those stupid movies. By the time we reached the car, I realized I hadn't heard another shot.

"Get in! Quick!" Still squatting, Dan reached up and opened the car door. I scrambled in, followed by Casper, then Dan. As we caught our breaths, Dan and I managed to keep our tongues inside our mouths, but Casper's hung down like a blown-out party favor. I patted her, wondering if the blast had scared her as much as it had me. I could feel her heart race beneath her thick fur.

After I stopped panting, I said to Dan, "Someone just tried to kill us!"

Dan shook his head. "I don't think so. I think they were trying to scare us off."

I frowned. "How do you know?"

Dan turned to me with that look.

"What?" I asked. "I didn't do anything!"

His eyes narrowed. "How about unlawful trespassing?"

I protested further. "I just *happened* to stumble upon what looked like a fortress or something, out in the middle of nowhere, and I was curious..."

He raised an eyebrow.

"...so I climbed up and had a look. Is that a crime?"

"Trespassing is," Dan said. "And it's dangerous when the property owners are paranoid pot growers."

"It's only a misdemeanor," I replied. "But I believe growing vast amounts of marijuana is a felony."

"Skunk," I said to Dan, pulling my hand back over the top of my head once we were back at my newspaper office. In spite of the sniper—or whatever—Dan had bravely rescued my Chevy by pushing it out of the ditch with his Jeep Cherokee. He'd followed me back to Flat Skunk, more to make sure I didn't get into any trouble than to see me back safely.

"Yeah, it stinks." Dan scrunched his nose as he rested the phone near his ear. He'd been on hold for five minutes, waiting for the hospital to connect him to Sheriff Mercer. "It always smells like skunk around here. If it isn't the skunkweed, it's the flattened roadkill in the middle of the road. That's why they call this place Flat Skunk, remember?"

I pointed to the website on my computer screen. "No. I mean, 'skunk' is a nickname for marijuana. Interesting." I returned to my screen and read the rest of the information I'd pulled up. After a few minutes, Dan put down the phone and waved in my peripheral vision to get my attention. At least he wasn't throwing snowballs.

"I'm going over to Mother Lode Hospital, check on the sheriff. You want to come?" He literally signed, "go," "hospital," "see," "cop," "you," and "come." He added the question mark at the end by raising his eyebrows.

Holding up a finger to indicate "Give me a minute," I hit the "print" icon, then nodded. I turned to my dog, resting at my feet. "Casper, you stay here. They frown on dogs in the hospital, even if you have the legal right to be there."

Casper looked at me as if I'd torn out her heart, stomped on it, and fed it to Dan's cat. She laid her head on her paws, those droopy eyes watching as I refilled her water bowl, added an extra helping of chow to her food bowl, and fluffed her dog bed in the corner. "Good girl," I said just before I closed the office door. If she really needed to leave, she could always use the doggy door I'd added at the bottom. And she was trained to go home if I wasn't around.

"You want Cujo to keep her company?" Dan asked, stopping by his own office to retrieve his jacket and check on his adopted watch cat.

"Very funny. My dog would be nothing but puffs of fur after your cat finished with her. Besides, Cujo creeps me out. Why do you keep him?"

"Like Casper, he's my signal cat."

I gave Dan a look. "There's no such thing as signal cats. Only dogs. Besides, can your cat obey commands? Like Sit, Stay, or Go home? Because Casper can. If I tell her to go home, she will."

"Even better. He responds to Eat, Sleep, and Get out of my chair. And he's really good at scratching bad guys."

"Not to mention his owner." I pushed up Dan's T-shirt sleeve. As expected, there were claw marks up and down his arms. Cujo had a disarming habit of leaping onto Dan from his perch on the file cabinet whenever he felt like it, kind of like Inspector Clouseau's houseboy, Cato.

"While we're at the hospital, you might want to have the emergency room doctor take a look at those wounds your attack cat made while keeping you 'on your toes'."

Mother Lode Hospital in Whiskey Slide had been undergoing a metamorphosis lately. With the influx of retirees, more beds were needed and new wings had been added, thanks to donations by wealthy relocated baby boomers who were rapidly aging the population. More surgery units had been added too, as well as a larger emergency room. However, the most popular wing at the hospital was the "P & M" wing—"preservation and maintenance"—which catered to those who couldn't let go of their youth just yet. Face lifts, liposuction, hair implants, and boob jobs topped the list of cosmetic surgery for those middle-aged and beyond, outnumbering gall bladder removals, knee surgeries, and hip replacements two-to-one.

As I walked the pink halls of the mammoth institution, I wondered if Sheriff Mercer would sneak over to the new wing for a remodel after his leg was mended. I'd never seen a man so frightened of growing old. Six months ago when I'd discovered the sheriff was going deaf, it had been a struggle to get him to be fitted for hearing aids. He'd been too proud, too stubborn—and too frightened—to admit his increasing disability.

Dan and I found the sheriff lying in his hospital bed, propped up on two large pillows, watching Dr. Phil. He muted the TV as we entered.

"Hey, C.W., hey Dan." The sheriff smoothed out his blanket, making sure everything that needed to be covered was covered—thank God. His right leg hung in a pulley-like contraption, in a cast from his upper thigh to his ankle. It had been signed by Taylor, Amber, and Devyn. Cute student nurses, no doubt.

"Wow, you look great!" I lied. He actually appeared pale, tired, and all of his sixty-something years. I handed over a gift bag full of sick-person goodies I'd picked up in the hospital gift boutique—copies of *Smithsonian* and *Field and Stream* magazines, five rolls of all-chocolate Necco wafers, a pair of Superman slipper socks, a moldable foam pillow, and the latest issue of *Eureka!*.

Dan pulled up a chair while I eased onto the foot of the sheriff's bed.

"So what does your doctor say?" Dan squirmed and glanced around the tiny sterile room. He seemed uneasy as if something might jump at him unexpectedly. I wondered what caused his discomfort. I'd never seen him like this.

The sheriff sighed. "It ain't broken, luckily. Doc says I'll be here a few more days though. Got a little infection, I guess. Anyway, then I'll get crutches or a wheelchair." He knocked lightly on his cast and shook his head. "I gotta wear this thing for six or eight weeks. How am I gonna get any work done like this, for Chrissake?"

"I'll handle everything, Chief," I said, channeling Lois Lane and patting his purplish toes. "Don't you worry."

"That's what I'm afraid of, C.W. You stay out of it. Let Arthurlene and my deputy handle things until I get out of here, you hear me?"

I tapped my ear and shook my head. "Sorry. No change. The doctors are not optimistic."

“You know what I mean, C.W.” His face colored, so I stopped teasing him.

“Seriously, any news from Arthurlene?”

He shrugged, eyed me, then spoke to Dan more than me. “She found evidence of drugs—marijuana, LSD, hashish. She’s doing tox tests to find out what else he might have taken.”

“So it could have been a suicide after all?” I asked. “Took a bunch of drugs, then jumped off the roof and hung himself?”

He shook his head. “I still think someone else was up there with him—”

We were interrupted by “Tiffany,” who arrived to give the sheriff his sponge bath. She looked eighteen or nineteen, too thin, too blonde, and wore her nurse’s outfit too short, too tight, and too open at the neck. It was the second time the Sheriff’s face reddened, this time for a completely different reason.

Once back at the Penzance Hotel building, I left Dan at his office after giving him a quick kiss and headed for my own office to get the new information into the computer for my pending story. Drugs, huh. I’d have to give Arthurlene a call for details.

As I inserted the key in the knob, I noticed the door was unlocked. Moving cautiously, I inched the door open, ready to bolt at the first sign of a disheveled office, a masked intruder, or a dead body.

What I found surprised the hell out of me.

A little girl sat at Miah’s desk, drawing a picture. She looked up, smiled her gap-toothed grin, and gave a tiny wave, a red marker still in her hand. She set down the marker and signed, “Hi, Connor,” using my familiar name sign—a “C” at the side of my chin.

Behind her, in a black leather bomber jacket, stood her dad, Josh Littlefield. My old boyfriend from Gallaudet University.

Uh-oh. Dan wasn’t going to like this.

# 7

"What are you doing here?" I signed without speaking, having temporarily lost the power of speech. With a quick glance down the hall, I closed the door to my office, hoping Dan wasn't planning to drop by any moment.

"Surprise!" Josh signed, flicking up his index finger near his eye. He handed me the flowers.

I took them and quickly set them on Miah's desk. Aware that Susie was watching my every move, I forced a smile. Being deaf like Josh and me, she was especially attuned to body language and facial expression. I didn't want her to think I wasn't glad to see her. On the other hand, I didn't know how I felt about seeing my old boyfriend from Gallaudet University.

Josh had come back into my life several months ago by accident. I'd been stunned to find him walking down the main street of Flat Skunk, signing to his hearing wife, Gail, and deaf daughter, Susie. They had come to the gold country to meet with a renowned audiologist and discuss the pros and cons of getting a cochlear implant for little Susie. Since Josh was deaf, he was against it. He didn't see anything wrong with being deaf and felt strongly about preserving Deaf Culture. Gail, who was a hearing CODA—Child of a Deaf Adult—wanted the surgery for her deaf daughter, hoping it would enable her to hear and be a part of the hearing world.

Unfortunately, Gail had ended up dead. I'd done my best to find her killer, which had nearly cost me my life. My relationship with Josh had nearly cost me Dan. Once Josh was out of our lives, Dan had proposed.

So what was Josh doing back?

Holding my smile steady for Susie's sake, I repeated my question, "I said, what are you doing here?" I moved to Susie and gave her a hug. She pointed to her drawing: A man and little girl standing by a disproportionately small house, holding hands. Obviously Josh and Susie. To the side was a woman lying down, her eyes closed, as if asleep. Susie's deceased mother, Gail.

I blinked back the tears I felt for Susie. I'd come to love her during the time we'd spent together while Josh was incarcerated, a suspect in Gail's death. I'd even had fantasies of her becoming my own.

"Surprised to see us?" Josh signed, grinning.

"No, I mean, yes...uh...but why are you here? I thought you were going to set up some sort of exclusive Deaf Community in the Midwest somewhere." I sat down in my office chair, feeling overwhelmed. Josh pulled up an extra chair and faced me. Susie went on with her drawing.

"That's why I'm here. I finally got the financing and just signed the papers. DeafTown is about to become a reality. Exciting, yes?"

I didn't know what to say. I thought he was crazy when he first came up with the idea of an all-deaf community. I'd heard there were such places, established by Deafies who feared the slow erosion of Deaf Culture. Thanks to improved testing, better health care, and the boon in cochlear implants, the deaf population was diminishing. Some deaf citizens felt threatened and wanted to preserve the unique culture they'd created. But these rare private communities weren't really self-contained. They were more like communes that still relied on the outside world for economic support.

"You're really going through with this?"

"Yes. You've heard of Laurent, South Dakota. Deaf people have incorporated a town there that's patterned after Martha's Vineyard of the 1800s."

I knew the history of the Vineyard—all deaf students did. Most of the citizens on the island were either deaf or knew sign language—a remarkably bilingual community. Unfortunately, it hadn't remained that way.

"Yes, but..."

"We'll have everything we need to be self-supporting. Stores, businesses, homes, churches, a community center, and a bilingual school."

"Wow. I can't believe it." I glanced over at Susie who was concentrating on her drawing. "That's always been your dream, ever since college. In fact, isn't that why we finally broke up? You wanted exclusion from the hearing world and I didn't. And then you ended up marrying a hearing girl."

Josh shook his head. "I don't think that's why we split, Connor. You got a job in San Francisco at the newspaper and I wanted to work in Washington, DC. Distance was the problem. But now that's changed. I realized when I saw you after so many years that I'd really missed you."

I tensed at his words. This wasn't what I expected. Or wanted. I thought Josh was out of my life and I didn't need this complication. Not with my already complicated feelings for Dan.

"So where's your DeafTown going to be? In the Midwest? Buying enough land to house a group of deaf people has to be expensive." Was there a sale on swampland in Florida? I wondered.

"Chinese Camp."

"Huh?" I crooked my index finger at him.

Josh nodded. "Chinese Camp. Right here in the Gold Country. We're going to be neighbors, Connor!"

Before I could scream, throw something, or smack him, my office door light flashed. Oh no! Not Dan. Panicked, I glanced at Josh and Susie, wondering if I could stash them under the desks or out on the window ledge. Josh, maybe, but not Susie.

Reluctantly, I moved to the door and turned the handle, dreading what I'd find on the other side.

It wasn't Dan. Thank God. Instead, the thirty-something man with a scruffy beard and glasses I'd seen in the diner now filled my doorway, wearing a puffy parka and snow-flecked *Sharks* hat. The "Big and Tall" shopper, about the size of the abominable snowman, had to be over six feet, pushing three hundred pounds. And he was frowning.

What now? Another angry "Letters to the Editor" writer demanding to have his say in print? The would-be assassin who tried to shoot me earlier? Even worse—another old boyfriend?

The man shifted his gaze from me to behind me. I turned to see Josh grinning. He saluted the man, "Hello."

"You found us. Good." Josh turned to me and signed rapidly, "C-O-N-N-O-R W-E-S-T-P-H-A-L, this is B-R-A-D-L-E-Y E-D-W-A-R-D-S. Brad, meet Connor, my..." He paused. I thought I saw him blush. "...My dear friend from college. Connor publishes the local newspaper."

Bradley Edwards reached out a mega-hand. I shook it, wondering if I'd be able to use my hand again, but his grip was gentle. I turned to Josh for further explanation. He apparently read my face clearly.

"Brad is the son of Dane Edwards, the financier of DeafTown. He's my partner." Brad gave him a look. "My business partner," Josh added quickly.

"Nice-meet-you," Brad signed without moving his lips. "Josh said many nice things about you."

I nodded, wishing I could say the same.

"So you actually bought the town of Chinese Camp? To turn into a deaf community?" I signed to Josh, still stunned at his news. "I know it's a ghost town, but it must have cost a fortune. And it's so rundown—you've got a lot of work and expense ahead of you."

"Like I said, the financing wasn't a problem," Josh signed. "The hardest part was convincing the realtor to sell the place to us. He was a little skeptical about turning the whole town over to what he called 'a bunch of deaf and dumb people.'"

I winced at the term. Luckily references such as "deaf and dumb" and "deaf mute" were dying out, but the prejudice still lingered. Some hearing people were suspicious of those of us who spoke with our hands, as if we were sharing secret information. Or were just plain freaks.

"I'm not surprised. The Gold Country seems to attract a number of subcultures. Most have a live-and-let-live attitude, but some are openly discouraged by the long-time residents from settling down here. The old-timers don't like change around here. And they especially don't like different."

"Well, I guess we'll sort of be like the Chinese settlers who used to live in Chinese Camp," Brad signed. "They weren't exactly welcomed either."

Apparently Bradley Edwards had been reading up on our local history. In 1849, thirty-five Cantonese miners arrived somewhat mysteriously and began prospecting the area. When the white miners pushed them out, and the Chinese gravitated to an area that lacked nearby water needed for placer mining. But the Chinese were patient, industrious, and hard working, and eventually produced nearly $2.5 million in gold. At one time Chinese Camp, known as "Chinee" and "Chinese Diggins," had stores, hotels, joss houses, blacksmiths, a church, bank, a Wells Fargo office, Masonic Lodge, and the Sons of Temperance. Today not much is left aside from some rickety buildings, abandoned mines, and a few tombstones.

"You won't be the only ones facing prejudice. I get letters from people who don't like the religious cults, bleeding heart tree-huggers, militant survivalists, even wealthy retirees and aging hippies here. The worst letters are about the new Gold Strike Casino run by a band of the Martis Indians."

"Really?" Josh frowned. "I'd think they'd welcome the influx of money to the area. After all, this is the *Gold* Country."

"Actually, it's just the opposite. The county gets nothing from the casino, but still has to fork out funds for increased traffic, pollution, extra police, things like that. And they're worried about bringing in the wrong kind of people—whiskey drinking, sin-loving gamblers—even though the casino doesn't serve alcohol or have 'adult' entertainment."

"I think DeafTown is sort of like the Indian reservation," Brad signed. "An exclusive community where Deaf people can live, work, and communicate in a silent world, without interference from hearing people. Just like the Indians preserving their culture while avoiding the influences of the White Man."

Uh-oh. If I thought Josh was an extremist, this guy was an uber-extremist. And did he really think deaf people could live without any interaction with the hearing world?

"In fact," Brad continued, "I feel a real sense of camaraderie with Indians."

I frowned. "Why is that?"

"We share a similar language—sign language." He tapped his chest with his thumb, hooked his index fingers together and raised them up, circled his ear with a flat hand, and rubbed the back of his hand with the other hand.

I blinked, uncomprehending, aside from one sign which resembled "friend" in American Sign Language.

He translated the Indian signs into ASL. "Me. Friend. Deaf. Indian."

Okay. Time to get these guys outta my office and back to their own dream world. I patted my chest, then wiggled my fingers, then pointed to Brad and Josh, and waved. Universal signs for, "Me. Type. You. Out."

Josh grinned and began collecting Susie. Relieved I would be getting some peace—I already had quiet—I headed for the door to let them out.

"Susie," I signed to the little girl, "come give me a hug. It's so great to see you!" She ran over to me, reached up, and wrapped her arms around my waist. As I hugged her back, my arm rubbed against something hard next to her ear. I pulled back, open-mouthed, holding Susie at arm's length.

Susie grinned and lifted her hair away from the side of her head.

"You got a cochlear implant!" I signed, tapping behind my ear with two bent fingers. "Wow!" I looked at Josh, stunned. "I can't believe it. Josh, you were so against the implant when you first came here. What changed your mind?"

As Susie let her hair fall back in place, Josh put a gentle hand on her shoulder. "It's what her mother wanted. It was the least I could do for her memory."

Tears sprang to my eyes. This was a side of Josh I thought I'd never see. Maybe he was changing—at least in some ways.

I gave him a hug, promised Susie I'd see her soon, and pulled open the door.

There, of course, stood Dan.

# 8

"Dan!" I said without signing. I could feel myself burn from my toes to my cheeks. I waved a hand toward Josh, then signed and said, "You remember Josh Littlefield. And his daughter, Susie." I gestured toward her.

Josh saluted "Hello" and stretched out his hand. Dan shook it briefly, nodding.

"And this is his friend...uh, Bradley Edwards."

Dan looked up at the big guy who dwarfed him and shook his hand.

I continued to babble like a nervous teenager. "Uh, Josh and Susie surprised me. I didn't know they were in town. I found them in my office, waiting for me."

I paused for a response from Dan—a nod, a smile, an "Is that so, Sweetheart?"

Nothing.

I rambled on. "He and Brad are buying Chinese Camp. The whole town. They're planning to turn it in to a community for deaf people. A DeafTown. You know?"

Dan gave a single nod, finally acknowledging me. At least I knew he could still hear. I was worried there for a minute.

"And Susie got a cochlear implant!" I turned to her and she lifted up her hair, proudly revealing what looked like a plastic button behind her ear.

Dan gave her a thumbs up.

"They were just leaving." I turned to Josh and widened the door. Dan stepped aside as the three made their way through.

"See-later, beautiful," Josh signed without speaking.

I glanced at Dan, hoping he missed Josh's signs. From his stone-faced expression, I couldn't tell.

I waved Dan in and closed the door as quickly as I could without appearing rude to the ones exiting.

"Whoa, that was weird." I shook my hair, then scratched a non-existent itch behind my neck. "I never expected to see him again."

Dan gave another brief nod. It either meant, "I believe you, Sweetheart" or "Yeah, sure, you big fat liar."

"Really," I protested. "He just popped in out of the blue."

Dan raised an eyebrow. "Just like that. 'Beautiful.'"

Uh-oh. "Yes, just like that."

His eyebrow lowered into a frown. Time to change the subject. "So, what's up with the autopsy? Find out anything?"

I sat down at my desk and Dan took Miah's seat. He swiveled as he talked, making his lips difficult to read. I reached out a hand to still him.

"The sheriff was right. According to Arthurlene, it wasn't suicide," Dan said.

Feeling the hairs on the back of my neck prickle, I leaned forward to focus on every word. "What did she find?"

"First of all, his pants pockets were loaded with all kinds of crap."

"Like what? Drugs?" I thought of the pot farm.

He shook his head. "A business-type card, shotgun shell, and another one of those bracelets the sheriff found on him."

Dan had started swiveling again. I put a hand on the arm of his chair to stop him. "Stop wiggling. You're making me dizzy and your words are all blurry. Say that again? A business card..."

He shrugged. "It wasn't exactly a business card. Same size, but there were some religious quotes printed on it. Some bullshit like '...Welcome the New Millennium, sayeth the Lord...' On the bottom was an Internet site—www.NewMillenniumChurch.com—and the names Big-Ruth and Little-Ruth Carter, His Messengers."

I nodded, familiar with the card. Grabbing a pad and pen, I jotted down "business card," then crossed out "business" and replaced it with "religious." Next to it I wrote the Carters' names and added a question mark. "So Zander must have known the Carters. Maybe he was a member of the New Millennium Church. Could be a clue."

Dan pulled a card from his pocket and held it up.

Eyes widening, I asked, "Did you take the evidence?" As a former ex-cop, Dan never broke the law. He left that up to me.

He shook his head. "This one's mine."

I took the card from his hand and looked it over. It was crumpled as if Dan had been using it like worry beads. "Don't tell me you've joined their so-called church?"

He laughed. "Not a chance. Those two 'church ladies' hand out their cards to everyone they pass. I'm surprised you don't have one."

I thought for a moment, then reached into my backpack, burrowed around a few seconds, and withdrew an identical card. "Okay, so they give them out to everyone. Guess it's not much of a clue. Anything else?"

"A shotgun shell."

I blinked, then wrote down the words. "That sounds promising. Any other shells found on the roof? Or bullets?"

"Nope. And the shell was a blank—the kind the Clampers use for parades and plaque dedications."

E. Clampus Vitas was notorious around the Mother Lode, but more for their colorful clothing and bad boy behavior than actual law breaking. The red-shirted, black-vested, shotgun-toting men were Gold Country originals, having formed their gender exclusive "club" back in 1851, originally to help "widders and orphans—mostly widders..."

They were essentially harmless—except for Kenny-Wayne Johnson, who'd broken from the group and formed his own para-military posse, the American Mutineers. They spouted the usual anti-government propaganda and right-wing supremacy. Members often sent semi-literate Letters to the Editor raging against invading Indian casinos, tree-hugging eco-terrorists, pot-smoking hippies, bleeding-heart animal lovers, and left-wing liberals—AKA Democrats. These "fringe" elements were apparently threatening the American Redneck way of life. Most of us just ignored them.

But could he have murdered Zander because of his anti-American hippie ways?

I put the name "Kenny-Wayne Johnson" next to "shotgun shell" and added another question mark. Soon there would be more question marks than clues.

"Alright. Anything else?" I bit the end of my pen, hoping it would help me think.

"The bracelet."

"I don't suppose this one was made up of Tiffany diamonds or those Italian charms?"

"Nope. More woven pine needles."

I nodded. "With a white flower, right? So why would Zander have a bracelet on him? Maybe it was a gift for India?" Remembering all the crafts hanging from India's eaves, I added, "Are you sure it wasn't hemp?"

"Arthurlene said pine needles."

I wrote down "Pine needle bracelet—white/yellow flower." A light went on. I'd noticed someone wearing a similar bracelet recently. Could have been made out of pine needles. I tried to picture the bracelet and the wrist that sported it. An image formed. Thin arm. Creamy youthful skin. A henna design painted on the back of the hand.

Mariposa Sunshine—or whatever her name was. I remembered she sold hand-crafted jewelry like that at the Farmer's Market.

I wrote her name down next to the bracelet and added another question mark. What did Mariposa have to do with Zander Nicholas, other than the fact that they were both nature lovers?

"Did Arthurlene say anything else? About the autopsy?"

"Zander definitely died of strangulation. But he had scratches on both sides of his neck, like he'd tried to fight it. And yes, there were drugs in his system—weed, LSD, hash. No surprises there. And not enough to kill him."

I added the word, "Drugs," next to Zander's name. "That's it?"

"No. He'd also taken Halcion and Valium."

"Sedatives? He would have been pretty asleep, then." I thought a moment. "Any cash?"

"No mention of any. Why?"

I tapped the pen on my desk, trying to make some sense of Dan's information. "Well, we found that big pot farm not far from his place—and well hidden from view, I might add. Planes flying over wouldn't have noticed it, even using infrared. Maybe he wasn't just growing a little grass for personal use."

Dan shrugged. "Then where's the money? He should have been living the high life, so to speak. But instead he's in a dump in the middle of Podunk Nowhere. Did you see a big satellite dish on the roof? A Winnebago in the driveway? A swimming pool out back?"

I stuck out my lower lip. It helped me think. "Maybe he used the money for something not so obvious."

"Like what?"

"Like, I don't know. But something. And maybe he cheated someone, some drug lord he was dealing with."

"Drug lord? You've been reading too many captioned films from the eighties, Connor."

"Whatever. I have a hunch Zander's death has something to do with his pot farm."

"*If* it was his."

"I'm sure it was," I said firmly. "It was near their property. And who else could have tended to it out there besides him and India?"

"If that's true, who did he sell to? The entire population of Flat Skunk couldn't inhale that much pot."

"Good question. I think it's time to visit to the boonies again. Wanna come?"

"Connor, have you forgotten the last time you were there? Someone shot at you."

"But like you said, they were probably just trying to scare me away. I'll be more careful this time."

"You and the word 'careful' don't belong in the same sentence."

I switched off my computer, tapped my leg to get Casper's attention, then raised an eyebrow at Dan. "Are you coming or not?"

"Yeah, I'm coming. It'll save me a trip, since I'd probably have to come rescue you anyway. Besides, I might need to take samples."

"Samples of...ha! I hope you're kidding."

Dan gave a lop-sided grin and stroked his salt and pepper beard. "Gotta verify what he's been growing before we go any further. Could just be parsley, you know."

"I know marijuana when I smell it," I said.

"Oh really?" Dan said. "Ever inhaled?"

"Of course. In college. Once."

"What happened?"

"I had a bad experience. I don't like to talk about it."

He pressed on. "Hallucinations? Paranoia? What? Tell me."

I shrugged. "After I smoked a joint, I ate a whole bag of barbecued potato chips, a carton of macaroni salad, a chocolate donut, and a chilidog."

"And..."

"Then I threw up."

# 9

"Casper, hop in!" I signed as we piled into my '57 Chevy. We took my classic car because Dan likes to drive it and because I can read his lips better when he drives. But over the bumpy snow-covered terrain of Poker Flat Road, it was hard to communicate. I spent the time jotting down questions I planned to ask India. After I snooped around a bit, of course.

A few yards before we reached the cottage, I pointed to snow-laced evergreen bushes on the far side of the road, well out of sight, to use as cover. I wanted to surprise India—and her dogs. At least I might make it to the porch this time, if not inside the door.

"Park here. I don't want India spotting the car if she happens to drive by. That'll give us a chance to look around the property and discover any more interesting hiding places."

Dan shook his head but did as I asked. Since my Chevy is a red and white two-tone, I could only hope the overgrown shrubs and plow-created snow mounds would be enough to hide it. Otherwise it would stick out like a deaf person at choir practice.

"Guess we should have brought your black SUV," I said as I rolled down the window so Casper could get some air. I gently closed the passenger door. "It's easier to camouflage."

"Good point," Dan said, after closing the driver's door and coming around to my side of the car.

I signed to Casper to stay in the car and not make any noise, but kept it simple: "stay" and "quiet" in dog sign language. She drooled and licked her chops.

"Good girl," I signed, then zipped up my padded hoodie and we set out on foot toward India's place. We crept to within a few feet of the cottage, keeping to the shrubbery. Each time I lifted my Uggs out of the snow, I wondered if they made a sound. Dan didn't hush me, so I assumed I was being quiet. But it didn't take perfect hearing to see the footprints I was leaving.

I tapped Dan, and signed, "Dogs there. Hear barking?"

Dan shook his head.

I was headed for the cottage, hoping to get a glimpse inside a window, when Dan grabbed the hood of my jacket and pulled me back into the bushes. I nearly fell on my ass.

"What—" I started to sign.

"Car," Dan signed, his gloved hands steering an invisible wheel. He pointed back the way we came. Maybe hearing did come in handy once in a while.

I crunched down further out of sight and strained to see. India was getting a visitor? Maybe someone offering condolences? This should be interesting. I didn't think the reclusive Zander and India socialized much, living way out here.

Moments later a car pulled into view. An SUV, black, of course. The Gold Country was overrun by them, so to speak. And since ninety per cent were black, I could hardly tell one from another. I peered from my hiding place, hoping to see who was driving the gas-guzzler, but the windows were tinted extra dark—probably illegally—and I couldn't see inside.

We watched the SUV pull up to the cottage and stop. Seconds later, the driver's door opened. Out stepped Kenny-Wayne Johnson in full army fatigues. Probably purchased secondhand from the old Army-Navy store in Bogus Thunder.

Another man exited the passenger's side, also wearing his military Halloween costume. Both looked around as if they were checking for spies before stepping onto India's porch. Kenny-Wayne rapped on the door four times.

India answered, her dogs at her side, their heads snapping up and down and tails whipping back and forth in a frenzy. Kenny-Wayne and his buddy took a step back. Then India gave a command to the dogs and they suddenly calmed. It wasn't easy to read her lips so far away, but it looked like the same command she'd used earlier: "pa-lay" or "ba-lay."

Kenny-Wayne and his sidekick entered the cottage, stepping carefully around the dogs. The door closed behind them. I looked at Dan, who looked as puzzled as I felt.

"What's up with that?" I signed, flipping my palms up, my middle fingers extended.

Dan shrugged.

"Should we get closer? Maybe I can peek in a window. Or you can hear them through the walls."

He shook his head and fingerspelled something. I pulled off his glove and signed, "Huh?"

"T-O-O R-I-S-K-Y," he spelled again.

I frowned. "Why do you think Kenny-Wayne is here? Come to comfort the widder?" I spelled "w-i-d-d-e-r." I stood up. "I'm going to take a peek inside his SUV."

"Connor, wait—"

Before he could grab me, I was out of reach. I came up behind the car and peered inside the window. Couldn't see a thing. I had a feeling they'd left the doors unlocked, figuring no one was around to break in. I tried the handle.

Bingo!

I stuck my head inside. Whoa.

The place was full of military crap. Haz Mat suits and gas masks. A Geiger counter. Brochures with words like, "self-reliance," "live free," "hazard analysis," "Cipro for anthrax." Jugs of water and freeze-dried food. About a hundred rolls of silver duct tape.

I didn't recognize everything but it all looked menacing. A cross between *Worst-Case Scenario Survival Handbook* and "Survivor."

I caught Dan waving in my peripheral vision. He nodded toward India's door.

I ducked down, closed the door slowly, and darted behind the SUV.

Kenny-Wayne and his buddy stepped out on the porch.

Leaving? Already?

It had only been minutes.

I stayed down behind the car, hoping they couldn't see me. Moments later I felt the car start up and saw the exhaust spew from the pipe. Scrunching down and hoping the SUV didn't back up, the tires spun and the car lurched forward, down the slick road, spitting snow as it went. I slowly stood up, making a mental note of the SUV model and license plate before it disappeared from view. Suburban with a vanity plate that read: "AMER MUT"

I glanced over at the cottage door. Closed. No sign of India.

I ran back to Dan.

"What the hell happened in there?" I signed to Dan.

"What the hell were you thinking?" he signed back.

I ignored him. "Think we should see if she's all right? Maybe Kenny-Wayne killed Zander last night, and just now finished the job by killing India."

Dan rolled his eyes and said, "Not really the same M.O., do you think?" I could almost see his words take shape in the frosty air.

"So? Not every killer repeats the exact same crime each time. Especially stupid killers. And if Kenny-Wayne did it, maybe he thinks he can get away with anything just because he wears camouflage." I kept half an eye on India's door as I signed and spoke to Dan. "Remember that shotgun shell Zander had in his pocket?"

"Yeah. That's enough to hang him," Dan said, shaking his head. "What's his motive?"

"I don't know. Maybe Zander hurt his feelings or something. So Kenny-Wayne decided to take him out."

"Or maybe he was here to buy some dope," Dan offered.

"Oh, the old 'Keep It Simple, Stupid' rule?"

"I'm just saying, if it walks like a skunk, talks like a skunk..."

"...then it probably stinks. You really think Kenny-Wayne was here buying grass? Does he look like the pot-smoking type to you? I'd classify him as more the tobacco-chewing, beer-guzzling, glue-sniffing type."

I glanced back at India's door. "I still think we should check on her. I'm gonna peek in one of her windows, see if she's okay."

I started to get up. Dan pulled me back down. This time I did fall on my ass. And now my ass was wet.

"What now!?" Exasperated, I sliced my index finger sharply across my other open palm.

Dan had turned toward the road. With a finger to his lips, he gave me the universal sign for "Shut up."

I couldn't believe my eyes. Down the road came the black SUV.

"He's coming back!" I signed to Dan. Hmmm, I thought, if Kenny-Wayne did something, was he stupid enough to return to the scene of the crime? If there had been a crime.

I had a sudden, terrifying thought. Maybe he'd spotted my not-so-subtle Chevy not so hidden in the bushes.

"Down!" Dan signaled. We both pulled back behind the bushes and squatted in the snow. My butt got colder. We'd been out in the weather too long and the chill had seeped through my California-style winter clothes.

As the black Suburban slowly drove past us, it morphed into a black Pathfinder. Not Kenny-Wayne.

Someone else.

The car windows weren't tinted, but I still couldn't see inside. They were all fogged up. Damn!

We watched as the SUV pulled up to the front of the cottage. Both doors opened simultaneously. Two large blue-cloaked figures stepped out, leaving the doors ajar. I glanced at the license plate.

"TNKULRD."

Good old Californians. They loved their personalized plates. First AMER MUT—Obviously "American Mutineer." Now TNKULRD. "Thank you Lord"—at least a little more challenging. But thanks to fingerspelling, deaf people had an advantage reading words with missing letters and were used to filling in the blanks. The real question was, what in God's name, so to speak, were the New Millennium evangelists doing at Earth Mother India's place?

Little-Ruth and Big-Ruth Carter lumbered up the steps to the front door, hugging their hooded cloaks tightly around them. I didn't see any religious propaganda in their hands. No leaflets. No Bibles. Actually, I couldn't see their hands at all, tucked inside their sleeves.

Hmmm, something up their sleeves? I wouldn't doubt it.

Once again India opened the door, shotgun-free and her dogs quickly at ease. She waved the pair inside and they entered without a backward glance.

I turned to Dan, even more puzzled than before. He flipped his palms up, indicating that he, too, was totally confused with the comings and goings at the cottage in the woods.

I was getting leg cramps, frozen fingers, dry lips, and a chapped ass. Soon I'd be a human Popsicle. I couldn't take much more of this surveillance stuff. Luckily I didn't have to. Once again, the door opened. Only a few minutes had passed. Whatever was going on in there apparently didn't take long. Maybe India wasn't ready to accept the Carters as her saviors. Maybe the Carters just wanted to drop off a casserole. Or maybe the three of them had just made a deal. A drug deal.

The two super-sized women made their way back to their truck, hands still tucked in their sleeves. Once inside, they pulled the doors shut. With a puff of exhaust, the vehicle took off down the road, careening from side to side on the slippery surface.

I looked at Dan, open-mouthed and dumbfounded.

"Well," he said, "at least we know India is still alive."

"But we don't have a clue what's going on at Grand Central Cottage. And it's driving me nuts!"

"Look, Connor, I'm freezing out here," Dan signed. He pulled his gloves on over his reddened hands.

"Likewise," I signed, moving the manual letter "Y" back and forth between us. "Let's go. Next time I need to dress in four more layers."

"Next time? What next time?" Dan said, as we started for my hidden Chevy. "We're not coming back out here. There's no point."

"But we learned something, didn't we?"

"What? That India has friends?"

"Friends who don't stay very long. It's like a crack house out here, with all the in-and-out visits."

Dan frowned. "You think the church ladies could be buying dope from her, too?"

"Possibly...for 'religious reasons.' Maybe it helps them 'see the light.'"

"You could be right. Or maybe that's how they recruit new members." Dan lifted a questioning eyebrow.

"Well, I'm coming back. Tomorrow. I have a few more questions I need to ask India. But right now I need a warm bath, a hot drink, and a little massage to thaw this bone-numbing chill." I grinned at him coyly.

"Sounds good. How about I run the bath water, make some hot chocolate, and—" Dan turned his head, alert as a deer.

I shook my head. "Oh, no," I signed. "Not again—"

Dan pulled me behind the bush that hid my car. An instant later another black SUV appeared in view, heading toward us. Through the shrubbery I watched the car speed by, and managed to spot the make and license as it drove past.

This one was a Yukon.

The vanity plate read "DEFTOWN."

Oh my God.

# 10

*Josh?*

It couldn't be.

I looked at Dan.

"O.K.," he signed, shaking his head. "We'll go back. But just to check out who's in that car."

We marched as quickly as the thick snow would allow, still keeping to the bushes. At this point I was freezing, but nothing would stop me from finding out who was in that Yukon.

The truck appeared to be empty by the time we arrived back at our vacated hiding place in the bushes. Damn. We'd have to wait to find out who was inside. If these visitors followed the pattern, they'd be back out any minute.

I could feel Dan's eyes on me instead of India's door, but I didn't return his look. I sensed it was an "I told you Josh was a loser" look. After a few minutes, though, I couldn't take the stare-down any longer.

"What?" I flipped my palm up.

"Nothing. Just wondering what's going on in that head of yours."

I pinched my throat, the sign for "curious."

Dan nodded. Smugly.

Before I could smack him, I caught sight of India's door opening. Riveted, I peered through the bushes, ignoring the cold that numbed my extremities.

Two big and tall figures stepped out and closed the door behind them. They were covered from head to foot in snow gear, making it hard for me to see their faces. One wore a heavy leather jacket, fringed at the bottom and along the sleeves, with a leather cap pulled down over his eyes.

Not Josh.

The other guy, also not Josh, thank goodness, was bulky even with all the layers of clothing. He wore a Sharks hat. It was Josh's Yeti friend, Bradley Edwards.

What was *he* doing at India's?

Neither of the men appeared to speak. Or sign. I wondered if the other guy was deaf too. Edwards headed for the driver's seat while Leatherman pulled open the passenger door. As Leatherman turned his back to me, I recognized him instantly by the long black braid he wore down his back.

Dakota Goldriver. Chief of the Martis Indian tribe. CEO of the Gold Strike Casino.

It looked like Brad Edwards had meant what he said about deaf people and Indians having a connection. It appeared these two had something in common. But other than minimal sign language similarities and perhaps a history of oppression, what could their relationship be? Was this about drugs? Gambling? DeafTown? Or something else?

As the truck drove off, my heart skipped a beat. I thought I saw a shadow move in the back seat, but I couldn't be sure through the foggy windows.

*Josh?*

I looked at Dan and pinched my neck twice. Curiouser and curiouser. Damn it.

"Finished!" Dan signed, as he headed back to the car. I followed, trying to convince myself that the concept of "cold" was simply mind over matter. But I had another matter on my mind, and I was shivering even with the heater on. As we drove back toward town and my diner/home to thaw, I envied Casper her thick white coat.

After a hot bath for two—and a little time with my favorite bath toy—we cozied up in white terrycloth bathrobes from the "Mark Twain Slept Here" Bed and Breakfast Inn, a gift from Beau Pascal, owner of the B&B. He had given them to me for solving a murder that had occurred on the premises.

Dan, Casper, and I stretched out on the unfolded sofa bed, humans holding mugs of chocolate, dog enjoying a chew toy that looked like a chocolate bone. I switched on the captioned news and read the headlines while Dan listened.

The Zander Nicholas homicide wasn't exactly the lead story out of Sacramento's national affiliate station. Finally, after a dramatic opening spiel by a male-model-turned broadcaster, Sheriff Mercer appeared on camera from his hospital bed.

"I can't discuss the case," the sheriff said, his hair neatly combed, his face freshly shaved. Was that makeup he was wearing? He looked better laid up than he did on the street. What a ham.

"Were you hurt in the line of duty?" the reporter asked.

Sheriff Mercer's face reddened. "No comment."

I giggled. If they only knew he had fallen on his ass just walking down the street. He'd never live it down.

Using way too many facial expressions, the reporter summarized his information, which wasn't much. Zander was murdered. The motive was unclear. There had been no arrests. More at eleven.

Dan switched off the TV and the lamp next to him.

I switched on the lamp by me and reached for my notepad.

"You're not going to work on that now, are you?" he asked. I felt his warm feet caress my toes. His foot began to creep up my leg. At least, I thought it was his foot.

"Wait! Wait! I want to go over my notes while everything's fresh in my mind."

I flipped open the cover and scanned the question marks. That was about all I had besides a flimsy list of suspects.

Dan pulled his feet away, put his arm behind his head, and stared at the ceiling.

"I'll only be a minute. So what do you make of the parade at India's today? Think they were there to give their condolences?"

Dan shrugged. I couldn't tell if he was sulking, bored, or deep in thought. Maybe that's why I loved him so much. While other hearing people's body language is generally easy to read,

Dan was the exception. An enigma, wrapped in a sexy leather jacket—

I didn't get to finish my thought. Dan leapt out of the bed, stark naked. Casper's head began snapping. Both focused their attention on the back window.

I froze.

Something was in the backyard.

"What is it?" I signed using my index finger to make a question mark, but was ignored. Dan grabbed his jeans, pulled them on without buttoning them, and stepped into his boots. Seizing his jacket, he reached into the pocket and withdrew his gun.

"What are you doing?" My index fingers and thumbs tapped together rapidly.

Dan ran to the kitchen and returned with a flashlight. Shushing me, he headed out the front door, Casper right behind him.

"Casper!" I yelled. "Come!"

She hesitated at the doorway and glanced back at me, then followed Dan as he disappeared into the darkness. I didn't know whether to praise her for being a good watchdog or chastise her for disobeying me. Not the time to worry about it.

I grabbed my robe and wrapped it around me, hoping I'd feel less vulnerable. I needed a weapon to defend myself, in case the prowler—if that's what it was—somehow got past Dan and Casper. I reached for the handiest thing in sight: the remote.

What was I going to do with a remote? Change the bad guy's channel? I threw it down and ran to the bathroom. Inside the medicine chest I found enough spray bottles of knockoff cologne, discount deodorant, and power hair product to blind a dozen prowlers.

I took all three, slipped the cologne in the pocket of my robe for backup—knockoff or not, it had still been expensive—and held the other two at eye level, aimed and ready to blast.

I headed for the front door and peeked out.

No sign of Dan or Casper—not even the beam of Dan's flashlight. Just darkness. They must be at the back of the house.

Inching along the side of the house, I peered around the corner.

Nothing.

Feeling the hairs on the back of my neck tingle, I took a few more barefoot steps in the snow, unaware of the cold. My trigger finger ached, poised to shoot the spray at a second's notice. When I reached the back corner of the wall, I stopped, hoping for some sign of Dan's light.

More darkness. Not even a moon.

I peered around the corner, blinking to help my eyes adjust to the night. I stepped forward and felt something beneath my bare foot. Warm flesh.

"Dan!" I dropped my weapons and knelt beside him.

He lay face down in the snow, his flashlight dark near his outstretched hand. Casper stood nearby, her tail wagging furiously. She held something in her mouth.

Putting a hand on the side of Dan's head, I felt something sticky. I grabbed the flashlight and switched it on, praying it would work. The light flickered and danced around the snow, the reflection nearly blinding me. I turned the beam on Dan's face.

And saw blood.

"Dan! Dan!" I said, gently rubbing his shoulder.

I was about to lean over and give him mouth-to-mouth when he started to move.

I sat up. "Oh thank God! Are you all right?"

He rolled over. His eyes fluttered open and he squinted at me. Lifting an arm, he covered his eyes.

"The light..."

I moved the beam away from his eyes. "Oh, sorry. I just...oh, God! I'm so glad you're okay. Can you sit up? I'll call 911."

He rose up on one elbow, scrunching his face in pain. Slowly, gently, I helped him to his feet and led him back inside. Casper followed, nearly tripping us in her excitement. She still carried something in her mouth. I hoped it wasn't Dan's gun.

When we got inside, Dan refused the 911 help. I cleaned the blood from the side of his head, revealing a superficial gash.

Someone had hit him. Hard. Not forceful enough to kill him, but enough to make him fall and disorient him temporarily. Luckily Dan had a hard head. Something he accuses me of having.

I stuck a couple of Super Hero bandages on his temple, then said, "We've got to get you to the hospital, and call the sheriff, and—"

Dan held his hand up. "No. I don't need a doctor and the sheriff is laid up, in case you've forgotten. Really, I'm fine."

I made the sign for "stubborn," the same sign as "donkey"—my hand at my temple, bent down like an ear—and sat back. "All right, then, what happened?"

He touched the bandages. "Stupid. I should have been more alert. He surprised me from the back. Shit, Connor. What the hell's going on?"

My back stiffened. Good question. Aside from the fact that someone had been on my property, I had no clue.

Casper, whom I'd been ignoring in favor of Dan, finally dropped the object she'd been carrying at my feet. I patted her, pleaded for forgiveness for neglecting her, and called her a hero, my precious angel, and shoogy-woogy-honey-bear.

Then I bent over and picked up the shiny gift she had had brought into the house. It looked like a palm-sized anchor made of metal, painted red, with a hole at the end. I almost missed the blood on the tip of one side.

I held it up for Dan. "What the hell is this?"

# 11

Dan took Casper's find from my hand and looked it over.

"Looks like some kind of rope pulley," Dan said. He examined the tip. It still held traces of blood. "By the way, you shouldn't have touched it."

"You touched it too!" I protested. But he was right—I hadn't been thinking about fingerprints. "I thought it was one of Casper's gifts. She's always bringing in strange things from outside. I didn't know it might be the weapon that knocked you out."

He shot me a look. "I wasn't knocked out."

I gave a short laugh.

"I wasn't! I...lost my balance when I got hit and...sat down. That's all."

"You were lying on the ground, out cold. If it hadn't been for me—"

He sat up on the sofa bed, letting the damp cloth drop. "What? You think you rescued me? It's just a scratch. I told you—I lost my balance. I would've caught the creep if you hadn't come stumbling around the corner screaming my name!"

I fumed. Apparently I'd trod on his male ego. I guess he couldn't accept the fact that I might have saved *him*. Well, fine. I knew what it was like to be rescued when I didn't need rescuing. Hearing people tried it all the time, thinking my deafness was some sort of disability. Okay, so, it's a "disability," but that doesn't mean I need constant assistance.

I changed the subject. "So what was this rope thingy doing in my backyard? With blood on it? Someone obviously used it to...distract you..." Since it was already covered with Dan's and my fingerprints, not to mention Casper's slobber, I took it back, handling it freely. "What's it used for exactly? Rappelling in the local caves?"

"Could be."

"We're a long way from Moaning Caverns. Anything else?"

Dan frowned, which caused him to wince. He touched his wound. "Climbing. Rocks, mountains, trees, building facades..."

A shiver ran up my back. "Trees?" The digger pine, cedar, and oak trees in my backyard weren't strong enough to hold the weight of an adult.

"Maybe you were attacked by that tree-girl, Mariposa Sundial, or whatever her name is," I teased.

"Very funny," Dan signed, brushing two fingers down his nose. "What if I hadn't been here, Connor? What if I hadn't heard a noise outside? What would you have done?"

"Casper would have saved me. She's a vicious, man-eating beast—"

"She's a pussycat. And practically a vegetarian! You don't even let her have bacon."

"Well, maybe she would have licked the prowler to death."

Dan didn't smile, apparently not enjoying my witty repartee. It was time to shut up.

I switched off my light and snuggled up to him, feeling his body relax at my touch. He wrapped his arm around me and I lay on his chest, teasing his nipple and enjoying the rise and fall of his breathing. Leaving Casper to stand guard against future prowlers, Dan and I switched from sign language to body Braille. We're fluent in both.

The call to the cops could wait until tomorrow.

Over mochas the next morning, Dan and I talked about the events of the previous night. Actually I talked, he sort of listened.

"Think what happened last night had anything to do with Zander's death?" I asked after scanning the competition for details of the murder. The *Mother Lode Monitor* had about as much new information as yesterday's TV newscast. Good.

"Possibly," Dan said, studying the sports section. I read the headline upside-down: *Flat Skunk Clampers Clobber Bogus Thunder Moose at Horseshoe Competition.*

"Think my car might have been spotted yesterday out at India's?"

"Maybe," Dan said without looking up. Hearing people can do that—look at something else while they're listening.

"Think the Clampers might want me to do a striptease for them at their next meeting?"

"I suppose..."

I slapped his newspaper. "You might be hearing, but you're not listening!"

"Yes, I am. You said you're going to do a striptease for the Clampers."

Bastard.

"Seriously, Dan, you know that gizmo you got knocked...I mean, hit with. Maybe it really is Mariposa's. Didn't Arthurlene say the sheriff found something on Zander's body that tied her to him? A pine needle bracelet?"

"That's a pretty weak link, Connor. It doesn't prove anything."

I sighed and let Dan return to his newspaper. Flipping open my reporter's notebook, I wrote down a few "what ifs."

What if all kinds of people were buying dope from Zander Nicholas—paramilitary fanatics like Kenny-Wayne, religious cults like the New Millennium, casino Indians like Dakota Goldriver. Even deaf people like Bradley Edwards or Josh...

I let that thought drop.

What if someone killed Zander because of a dope deal gone wrong? What if he'd been dealing with the mob? Or some Colombian drug cartel. Or—

Now I was just recycling bad TV plots.

All right. Let's try another tack. What about cutting off the supply? That wouldn't have been smart. Unless the supply isn't cut off, thanks to India?

I was going around in circles. Time to stop speculating and do a little investigative reporting. I wanted to find out the connection between Zander, India, Kenny-Wayne, the Carters, and Chief Goldriver. Not to mention Bradley Edwards.

I got up from the table and put the mugs in the sink.

"Where are you going?" Dan asked, folding up the newspaper.

"Out," I said. "I need to do some...shopping."

Dan raised an eyebrow. He was too good at reading my face. I must have some kind of "tell," like poker players. I'd have to work on my lying and deceptive look if I was ever going to play poker with him. Which reminded me—I needed to pay a visit to the Gold Strike Casino. Since Zander had a token from the place, it might be the key to everything. Like it's going to be that easy.

I thought about the letters to the editor I'd been receiving. Citizens in the Gold Country had initially welcomed the casino, figuring it would bring more money into the historic area. But in recent weeks the tone of the letters had turned hostile. Writers complained that the casinos were actually taking money away from the county, not contributing to it. The casinos required more policing, more medical assistance, more emergency room care, more time from local political leaders. But since they had been built on Indian land, they weren't required to pay taxes on their income.

I'd have to do a little gambling to see what I could find out.

Rifling through my clean laundry pile, I layered up in black jeans, long-sleeved "Parental Discretion—Strong Language" T-shirt, "Sierra Nevada Breweries" hoodie, double-thick socks, and Uggs. As I grabbed my backpack, I spotted the pulley.

The casino would have to wait, I thought. I stuffed the pulley inside my pack. I had a better idea.

Casper and I left Dan as he headed for the shower. I promised to meet him for lunch at the Nugget Café after my "errands." He said he planned to drop by the hospital to catch up with the sheriff, then do a little investigating of his own. He wouldn't give me the details, only his usual warning to "Watch yourself, Connor."

As if.

Casper and I hopped into my Chevy and headed toward Rattlesnake Hill. According to town gossip—mostly Jilda at the café—Mariposa Sunshine lived part-time in a giant tree in the Calaveras Sequoia Forest. The Gigantean Sequoias aren't as tall as the coastal redwoods, sometimes reaching two hundred to three hundred feet, but the trunks are larger, nearly twice the size, thanks to a term I loved called "butt swell," which can create a diameter of nearly thirty feet at the base. It reminded me not to sit for long periods or I'd get my own butt swell.

The tree she occupied, which she had dubbed "Tall Mother," was actually three trees that had grown together, forming a unique "tree house," perfect for tree-sitters to inhabit. It should be easy to spot.

As I drove along the snow-cleared road, I reflected on the article I'd written a few weeks ago on this eager college coed. Mariposa, a name she adopted while taking Environmental Studies at Sonora State University, planned her tree-living experiment as part of her thesis. She was determined to prove that man, or girl, could live comfortably with Mother Nature—at least part time—without destroying it.

Apparently she couldn't make the commitment to full time. I frequently spotted her in town, having lunch at the Nugget, shopping at the funky boutiques, buying products that I was pretty sure contributed nothing to the environment, but probably made her hair shine and smell good.

When I'd asked her why she didn't live in the tree full time like other environmental activists like Julia Butterfly and Rainbow Starbux, she said, "I don't need to be with Tall Mother twenty-four-seven to make a point. Our symbiotic relationship continues, even if I leave her for a few hours each day. When I return to her, we embrace each other, share our daily adventures, celebrate our diversity, and provide for each other's needs."

When I asked what she gets from the tree that she needs, she responded with more ambiguous clichés: "Unconditional love. A sense of my place in nature. And rejuvenation."

Don't forget free rent, financial donations, and lots of publicity, I wanted to add, but didn't.

Still it was true.

She admitted she was writing a screenplay and hoped to get a Lifetime movie out of the experience. She'd decided Lindsay Lohan or Mandy Moore would be the best choices to play her. But not Britney Spears. Too shallow.

"Last question: What does the tree get from you?" I'd asked, grateful to be winding up the interview.

"Well, of course, unconditional love, too. A chance to relate intimately to a human being. And the opportunity to share her natural beauty with others." She'd held up some of her woven pine needle "jewelry"—a necklace, bracelet, and anklet—which she sold at the Farmer's Market at ten and twenty dollars a pop.

I wanted to ask her how "intimate" she had been with the tree, but decided not to go there. None of my business what happens between a consenting adult and a tree.

And then she went off, spewing environmental jargon that I'd heard before. "The environment was contaminated by the miners during the gold rush. Mercury and arsenic, by-product of prospecting for gold, entered the food chain. Farmlands had been impacted and severely damaged. Wildlife had been devastated as elk, bighorn, deer, bears, and other species were slaughtered in great numbers. Indians were displaced. And it was all affecting the environment today, the dysfunctional leapfrog development that threatened the historic area."

When I'd asked her what she wanted to see happen, she rattled off a list: "No urban sprawl. Secluded homes. Frontier attitude of freedom and individuality. No removal of forests for food crops or commercial development. No sirens or noisy neighbors. Leaves instead of pavement beneath our feet."

Where was diversity? A sense of community? Empathy for people as well as nature? NIMBY—Not In My Back Yard.

As I turned onto the dirt road that wound through the forest, I scanned the treetops for a sign of Tall Mother. Towering over the neighboring trees, she—it—was easy to spot. I drove slowly over the snowy road, hoping to find a place to park nearby. When I pulled closer, I leaned out the window and stared up at the natural monument in awe. Not only was it taller than the rest of the surrounding trees, but because three trees had merged into one, it was larger in circumference. Snow frosted the top branches, sheltering the lower ones and leaving them bare.

I stepped out to get a better look, freeing Casper to roll around in the snow. If I'd had any doubts about this being Tree Mother, I didn't once I got a closer look. Apparently Mariposa had "redecorated" her living quarters during the short time she'd been there. Tree Mother was adorned from trunk to tip—as far as I could see. Colorful scarves and ribbons fluttered from lower limbs. Windsocks flew from higher limbs. Parts of the trunk and several limbs featured stars, hearts, rainbows, sunflowers, peace symbols, and happy faces, all in eye-dazzling neon paint. Non-toxic, I hoped.

After taking in the extreme makeover, I searched for a sign of Mariposa. I spotted a large platform about thirty feet up, covered by an overhang, and figured that was her "flat." Brrr, I thought, feeling the chill through my layers. It had to get pretty cold up there at night. How did she keep warm?

I hated to drop in unannounced, but Mariposa said cell phones "hurt the Earth's oxygen," so I scanned the trunk for some kind of door chime or other way to alert her I was here. After a brief search, I found a cord attached to a pulley.

A pulley just like the one that Casper had found in my backyard.

Hooked to the nub of a broken branch at the bottom was a bucket with a pad of paper and a pencil and some clothespins inside. I scrawled a note announcing my presence, attached the note to the rope with a clothespin, and pulled the rope to move the note up to the platform. Bits of snow sprinkled down each time the clothespins brushed a nearby branch.

When the note reached its destination, I waited for Mariposa to peer over the platform and wave me up, or at least write a reply and send it down. No response.

Maybe she wasn't home.

Maybe I should go up and take a look, just to make sure.

Too heavy to hoist myself up using the pulley, I glanced around for some sort of elevator or stairs. Fat chance. Circling around the massive trunk, I spotted a ladder at the back, leaning against the tree. With bulky Uggs on my feet, it would be tricky climbing the slippery ladder.

What the hell.

I started up.

# 12

My foot slipped a couple of times, but the ladder held steady and I recovered quickly, holding tight to the rope. The only problem was I ran out of ladder about halfway up. Gazing up, I realized I still had another ten or twelve feet to go to reach Mariposa's quarters.

Now what?

I called Mariposa's name. No answer. Surely she could hear me from this distance. Maybe she was asleep. Or maybe she was hard of hearing. You never knew—deafness is an invisible disability. Anyone could have a hearing loss.

I looked up again, straining to see how far I had to go, and noticed a rope hanging down from a hole in the platform. Unlike the thin cord used to relay notes back and forth, this was a thick rope. Made out of hemp, as a matter of fact. Was this how Mariposa climbed the rest of the way up—via a rope? I grabbed hold of it, wondering if I was supposed to use the pulley-thingy in my pocket. If so, I had no clue how. Better stick to my wits—if I still had any.

I tugged on the rope. It held strong. Must be tied to the trunk or a sturdy branch near the platform. I studied the trunk. A number of limbs sprouted from it, some so thin they would easily break if stepped on, others gnarled and knobby that could serve as footholds. I grabbed the rope, looped it around my hand, and stepped onto a limb I thought might hold me.

Solid. I stepped on the next branch. So far so good. Only ten or twenty feet to go.

Could be worse, I thought, remembering a line from *Young Frankenstein*. Could be raining. Could be snowing. I felt a flake touch my nose. The wind had picked up, and a snow flurry was beginning. Great. My gloved hands were already cold. Soon they'd be wet, and then frozen solid.

Trying not to look down, I kept a steady pace, grabbing the rope and stepping on each slippery branch, pulling and pushing myself up, limb by limb. I broke one branch, but my foot slid down to a strong foothold below, and the rope kept me from tumbling to the bottom.

I was sweating bullets by the time I reached the platform. I stuck my head through the wheel-sized hole in the middle, feeling like a groundhog checking for signs of spring. No sign of Mariposa. She'd probably gone to town. It seemed a shame to waste all that effort, so I pushed myself the rest of the way through the hole. I sat down on a blanket that had been spread over the wooden platform while I caught my breath and pondered whether I could be arrested for "breaking and entering." I didn't think so. Besides, that had never stopped me before.

Great what you've done with the place, I thought, scanning the eclectic furnishings and decor. The blanket, spread over the platform, apparently served as her bed, with a pillow at one end, covered by a Strawberry Shortcake pillowcase. She also had a small refrigerator that ran on batteries, several Kerosene lamps, and some cardboard boxes full of clothes, toiletries, books, and writing materials. No TV, radio, fax, or laptop in sight. The platform was covered with a waterproof tarp, about three feet over my head.

I sifted through the books, noting the titles. You may not be able to judge a book by its cover, but you can often tell a lot about a person by her books. Her collection ran the gamut, everything from subversive literature to chick-lit romance novels. *Catcher in the Rye, Bridget Jones' Diary, The Eco-Terrorist's Manifesto, Kama Sutra, Medical Uses of Marijuana, Life and Times of the Beatles*, and several *Dummies Guides* on screenwriting, gambling, and romance.

An interesting library, to say the least. I wasn't sure what it told me, except that Mariposa Suncatcher wasn't exactly an open book. Sex, drugs, and rock and roll, not to mention gambling, ecology, and love. Odd. I thought she was just a college student looking to get an A.

I found another box with something more disturbing. Literature on E.R.T.H.—Environmental Repair That Heals—which promoted "sabotage, arson, and vandalism to attack everything from logging equipment to genetically engineered crops and SUVs." There were detailed instructions on how to create "incendiary devices" using "five gallon buckets filled with gasoline, diesel, wires, and kitchen timers."

Okay.

I peered over the side of the platform to make sure she hadn't come back and spied Casper, almost invisible in the falling snow. Luckily she had on her thick fur coat, just made for this type of weather.

"I'll be right down, girl," I called. Her tail wagged in response.

The snow was really starting to come down and I worried about getting stuck out in the forest if the roads became impassable. I rummaged through the box of clothes and pulled out a yellow slicker that might help cut down on the wind chill. Zipped up and temporarily comfortable, I snooped around in the box full of notebooks. Most seemed to be schoolwork, but the one on top looked like a journal. I flipped through a few pages and skimmed the entries—all reflections on living in a tree. Overwrought, flowery, and downright dull.

I stood up, ready to head down, and knocked over the box of books. I lifted up Salinger, about to return it, when I noticed how light it felt. Lifting the cover, I flipped through a few pages.

Most of them were glued together.

I ran my fingers over the top page. It gave under my touch.

I poked it. It tore.

The old hidden-money-in-the-cut-out-book trick. Basic Nancy Drew stuff.

I peeked inside the hollow, then turned the book upside down. Dozens of fresh hundred dollar bills fluttered onto the blanket.

Whoa. Where did Mariposa get all this money?

I gathered up the money and was about to stuff it back inside when I saw something stuck at the bottom. Using a fingernail, I dug it out. A snapshot. Four of them, in fact. Taken with a disposable camera. Not exactly "green" of her.

I studied the first one. It appeared to have been taken at a gambling table. It was a little blurry and the shot was taken from an odd angle. A secret camera? I wondered. Wouldn't put it past the amateur Girl Detective.

The picture focused on a man at a poker table hunched over a hand of cards. Behind him stood another man, his arms crossed in front of him. He had a scraggly beard, glasses, and a frown on his face that I recognized.

Bradley Edwards.

He wore a gold jacket with the Gold Strike Casino insignia—a stack of gold coins. Bradley worked at the casino? It made sense. He'd been with Dakota Goldriver at India's place.

I checked the next photograph. The same poker table but from a different angle. This time the photographer shot the picture from behind Bradley and the gambler, facing the dealer. Always looking for body language, I tried to interpret their faces. The dealer seemed to have his eyes on Bradley, not the gambler.

I checked the last two pictures. Bradley was in both of them. But like those "Can You Spot The Differences?" pictures in magazines, these snapshots were slightly different. Bradley still had his arms crossed in front of him—his right arm on top of his left—but his hand configurations had changed from picture to picture. I noticed because the camera was at waist level. And I'm especially attuned to people's hands.

In the first picture, the index fingers of Bradley's right and left hands were extended. In the second picture, the right hand appeared to shape the manual letter "P" or "K," while two fingers peeked out from the left. In the third, he seemed to be making an "F" or a "9" in his right hand, and a fist in the left.

I looked at them again.

Right hand: "1" or "D." Left hand: likewise.

Right hand: "P" or "K." Left hand: "U" or "H."

Right hand: "F" or "9." Left hand: "S."

Bradley's hands spoke, if not loudly, at least clearly, if you knew how to read them.

Ace of Diamonds.

King of Hearts.

Nine of Spades.

Bradley Edwards was signaling to the dealer.

They were cheating. Using sign language.

A spray of snow fluttered in, reminding me of my surroundings. I looked up. The platform was protected by a tarp, so I hadn't really noticed the increase in snowfall. Now it was blowing in from the side.

Time to get out of here.

I stuffed the pictures and money back into the book, wishing I could repair the page I'd torn. Mariposa was sure to know someone had been snooping in her stuff. But she'd wonder why there was nothing missing. And she'd sure as hell wonder who had been in her tree fort.

Replacing the book in the box, I scrambled to the hole in the platform and, feet first, slowly eased myself down. I wiggled my foot blindly, until it found a branch. Then I grabbed the rope and began my descent. As I neared the bottom of the rope, I looked down to locate the ladder. My heart dropped into my stomach.

The ladder was gone. I checked again to be sure. Gone.

Although the snow was really coming down, it wasn't windy enough to knock over that heavy ladder and bury it. Someone had taken it.

And it was at least a twenty-foot drop to the ground.

# 13

"Fuck!" I screamed. A few times. Until my throat hurt and I couldn't scream anymore. Exhausted, I leaned against the trunk, wondering if a person yells "Fuck" in the middle of the forest and no one is around to hear it, does it still help to yell it?

Fuck, yeah.

Temporarily recovered, I scanned the forest. Nothing but trees and snow as far as the eye could see. An enchanted ice palace—or prison, depending on how you looked at it. From up here, it didn't look good.

What now? I was up the tree without a ladder, so to speak. Beneath me, a twenty-foot drop. If I fell, I'd probably break both my legs, a couple of ribs, and all my fingernails. Not to mention the cuts and bruises I'd acquire on the way down, thanks to jutting branches with knife-sharp points. I could even poke an eye out.

Practically hanging by a thread, I was tired and cold and hungry and crabby. And I had to pee. I climbed back up to the platform to wait it out. Surely Mariposa would be back soon.

Surely.

I tucked my hands in my pants pockets and felt something.

My Sidekick. Yippee! I never went anywhere without it. I pulled it out. It would be my lifeline. Unless, of course, there was no reception out here in the middle of Antarctica. I switched it on and waited, holding my frosty breath.

Not only was there no reception, but I also had a dead battery. I shook it, hit it, and swore at it. Nothing. Great. Just great. I thought about having a tantrum and throwing it to the ground, but that was childish.

Instead, I cried.

When I finished with my tears, most of which had frozen to my face, I gave myself a good talking to. "You whiny, sniveling crybaby! You're not going to die up here. Someone will find you. Now get over it and start figuring out a plan, you weenie."

I stood and looked over my surroundings. The platform was carpeted with a blanket, loaded with boxes, and protected by a tarp overhead, sagging from the collection of fallen snow. In fact, the tarp was really starting to droop. I had a feeling any minute the whole thing would come down on my head and bury me in snow. Without the tarp, I'd have no protection from the oncoming blizzard.

The tarp.

I had an idea. The tarp was made of canvas, strong enough to weather the elements. If I could get it down, then tie it to the blanket...and the slicker...and whatever else I could find, I could make a "rope" strong enough to get me to—or at least near—the bottom.

I didn't watch old prison escape movies for nothing.

I reached up on tiptoe but the tarp was just out of range. I figured it was about eight feet—a bit taller than my five-feet eight inches. I jumped to see if I could push some of the snow off with my hand, but all I managed to do was bend my fingers back and nearly break the platform on my landing.

Not going to try that again.

I needed something—a stick or branch—to poke at the tarp to dislodge the snow. Then I could figure out a way to untie it or cut it down. After a brief scan of Mariposa's living quarters, I located a broom hanging from the nub of a broken branch. Who says you can't be a good housekeeper when you live in a tree?

In her "kitchen"—a box filled with basic eating utensils—I found a Swiss army knife. Jackpot! Thank goodness Mariposa had all the comforts of home. I noticed she even had a chamber pot in a far corner. At least I hoped it was a chamber pot. I really had to go.

After the most awkward toileting experience of my life, I was ready to attack the tarp. Using the end of the broomstick, I jabbed at the center of the makeshift roof, hoping to displace some of the ever-increasing snow. But the tarp was so full, the load so heavy, I barely dented it. I tried again, poking, pushing, prodding, hoping for a mini-avalanche. What I got was more like a dusting.

This wasn't going well. Time for Plan B.

I sank down, tired, frustrated, and wondering what Plan B would be.

Plan B. Plan B.

Okay, what if I managed to climb up high enough to reach one of the corners of the tarp and cut it loose? I'd have to duck so the snow would slide off the tarp without taking me with it. Then I could cut the other three ties, retrieve the tarp, and I'd be on my way down.

I studied the corners and the ties on the branches, and chose the most accessible one with the easiest branch to climb. Opening the knife to the largest blade, I stuck the blade between my teeth, pirate style, hoping I didn't cut my tongue out. I scanned the branch for a toehold, grabbed onto a higher branch, dug my foot into a notch, and stepped up.

Within seconds the rope that held the tarp in place was nearly within reach. If I stretched—and kept my balance—I could cut the rope. Probably. Maybe.

Carefully removing the knife from of my teeth, my lips frozen from exposure, I reached up and hacked at the rope—no easy task in my awkward position and with little leverage. After several minutes of backbreaking, hand-numbing slices, stabs, and cuts, the rope-tie split in half.

I ducked as the snow started down, then scrambled down to the platform to watch the mound slide past me.

Then it stopped.

I looked up. The tarp was still loaded with snow. I stood up and poked it again with the broomstick, then struck something firm. The branch, or whatever, seemed to be caught near the edge of the tarp, preventing the rest of the snowdrift from falling.

I stabbed the tarp again, trying to dislodge the branch. After a few jabs, I felt the obstruction give. It rolled, then tumbled off the corner of the tarp, striking me in the chest and knocking me on my butt. It landed at my feet on the platform.

I screamed.

A frost-covered Mariposa Sunflower lay next to me, frozen stiff.

I scrambled backward, crablike, to the far edge of the platform, nearly falling off. My heart was beating so fast, I thought I might pass out. The only thing keeping me together was the fear of taking a dive off the platform. That would kill me for sure.

Oh God. What now? Check to see if she was alive? Obviously she wasn't. Everything about her was icy blue, except her clothes, which were icy white. I couldn't see her breath in the cold air, and I could see mine clearly as I panted like a dog.

Mariposa was dead. And it sure didn't look like a suicide.

An accident? Maybe she fell? Trying to climb to the top of the tree? Lost her grip, hit her head on a branch, landed on the tarp?

I inched forward, thinking I might spot an obvious wound that would indicate an accident. Close, but not too close, I looked her over. Her long blonde hair was matted and covered her face. Using one finger, I carefully moved it out of the way—and wished I hadn't. Until then, the body had been just that—a dead body—which was bad enough. Now, after seeing her young face, the tragedy of her death hit me.

Poor Mariposa. Maybe she was a little kooky, but she believed in her cause. And it was a good cause—trying to save the trees, the land, the beauty of the Gold Country. After spending a few moments remembering her and respecting her reasons for being here, I took another look.

Had she fallen? Landing on a snowy tarp wouldn't have killed her. But if she hit her head on the way down, that could do it.

I peered at her scalp, looking for blood. Nothing except a few pine needles.

Remembering the pine needle jewelry she made, I checked her wrists. She wore a bracelet on her right hand, which was still decorated with henna designs. The other wrist was bare.

Carefully lifting her cold arm with my thumb and middle finger, I turned her hand over. It was stiff, not from the cold, but from rigor. I'd learned a little about rigor mortis from Arthurlene and the sheriff. It set in sometimes as soon as four to six hours after death and was usually gone by seventy-two hours, but it could be affected by weather. In the cold, rigor could be slowed considerably.

All I could deduce at this point was that she could have died as recently as four hours ago.

I was about to turn her hand back over when I noticed something shiny peeking out from between her tightly closed fingers.

Uh-oh. I had a hunch it was another token, just like Zander's. But I knew enough not to go fooling with evidence this time. As much as I wanted to make sure, I didn't want to break open her fingers to find out.

Besides, the sheriff would kill me.

I looked at her again, puzzled by her death and the possibility that she might be holding a casino token. Curious, I peered at her neck, which was covered by her hair.

Hidden underneath was a thin rope tied tightly around Mariposa's throat.

The girl had been strangled.

# 14

"I gotta get the hell out of here," I said to no one. Hopefully no one. If Mariposa was murdered—and it was looking like she was—the killer could still...be...out there...

I scrambled up and peered over the side. The drop was still too far to consider trying without the ladder. But I could go back to Plan B—tying materials together to extend the rope. I glanced up at the tarp and decided to forget it. Maybe there was something else lying up there that I didn't want to know about.

Carefully rolling Mariposa's body off the blanket, I tied the blanket to the end of the rope. That added another four or five feet. I glanced around for something else to use and spotted the box of clothes. After rifling through them, I chose the ones made from the thickest materials—jeans, sweatshirts, a jacket—and tied them to the end of the blanket. Another four feet.

Not enough.

What else could I use?

My own clothes.

Stripping out of my pants, sweatshirt, and jacket, I quickly tied them to Mariposa's clothes, hoping I didn't freeze to death in my bra and underpants in the time it would take me to get down. Brrrr.

I let the extended rope down through the hole in the platform, praying it would be long enough. Otherwise I was in real trouble. If the killer didn't come back to take care of me, I'd freeze to death. A fall might be a blessing.

*Don't think that way, Connor,* I said to myself as I grabbed the rope. Already shivering, I started my descent. Step by step, grasp by grasp, I made my way down the trunk of the tree, using footholds and holding the rope like the lifeline it was. My hands and feet stayed warm, thanks to gloves and boots, but my mostly naked body, arms, and legs froze. My hair whipped around in my face and stuck to my quivering lips. Only the sweat from the exertion kept me from turning into a human ice sculpture. For now.

When I reached the knotted clothing, I took a deep breath, then forged ahead, easing myself down while trying not to look at the ground beneath me. At one point my hair caught on a branch and I felt a handful of strands rip out. Several times I scraped my exposed stomach and legs. But after a while I became numb to the pain.

And then, as I took another step on a tree nub, I no longer felt the cloth between my legs.

I was out of rope.

I looked down at what appeared to be at least an eight- or ten-foot drop.

I had no choice.

I let go, screaming all the way down.

I opened my eyes, seeing spots, unable to breathe. Grunting, gasping, I tried to take a breath. My lungs wouldn't work.

As my vision cleared, I realized I was staring into another pair of eyes.

The creature licked me.

"Casper!" I could breathe again! Thank God, I'd just had the wind knocked out of me. What a horrible feeling, not to be able to catch my breath.

I hugged my dog. Her body felt warm next to my cold skin. "Come on, girl." I pushed myself up. "We've got to get out of here. Quick!" I ran to my car, Casper at my side, her head snapping, tail wagging.

"Thank God," I said to her as I wrenched open the door and dove inside. We huddled together for a few minutes, me using her for warmth, her using me for affection. "Okay, girl, I gotta start the car so we can turn on the heater and get the hell outta here."

I let go of Casper and scooted over to the driver's side.

My heart stopped as I looked at the ignition.

My car keys.

They were in my pants. The pants I'd used to help make my escape. Just great.

Tears sprang to my eyes.

I was still stuck.

In the middle of nowhere.

In a blizzard.

In my underwear.

Groggy, I opened my eyes. I must have fallen asleep, I thought as I lifted my head. I couldn't see out the windows—it was completely dark. Casper lay beside me, keeping me almost as warm as a fur coat. Thank God she was a big furry husky and not a little shorthaired dachshund.

*I'll freeze to death out here if I don't get help*, I thought. I knew there was no one around for miles. The rangers didn't even go out in this kind of weather. I thought about Mariposa, lying up in her tree.

Dead.

I remembered the photos and money I'd found.

Her killer could—would?—be back for the evidence any minute.

I had to do something or I'd die out here, one way or another. Yanking open the glove compartment, I hauled everything out, hoping for a flare, a spare key, a white flag even. Not a chance. Just a bunch of empty chocolate wrappers, a to-go coffee mug I'd bought at the Calaveras Frog-Jumping Jubilee, a dead flashlight, and half a dozen maps of the Mother Lode.

I slammed the compartment shut and pouted while I thought.

Grabbing the mug and a local map from the floor, I searched for a pen or pencil. No luck. I unfolded the map, located the sequoia forest, and tore that section out. Then I uncapped the insulated mug, stuffed the piece of map inside, and closed it up. All I needed was something to tie it with.

I looked around. No rope. No string. And fresh out of clothes.

Almost.

I still had my bra.

Reaching behind my back, I unhooked the bra and tugged at a strap. After a few attempts, the strap broke. I tied it around the coffee mug.

"Casper," I said to my dog as I hooked my bra around her neck, checking to make sure it was secure but not too tight, I opened the car door and signed, "Go home! Casper, Go home!" moving my fingertips from my chin to my cheek.

She licked me. Of course.

I shook my head and repeated the sign for home. "No, Casper. Go home! Go home!" I shoved her out of the car and into the darkness.

*Come on, Casper*, I thought. *You're as smart as Lassie. Smarter. You know sign language. You can do this.*

Of course, she'd never done it from such a distance.

I curled up in the back seat trying to get warm, and waited.

If a car drove up, I'd never hear it, but I'd see the headlights in the dark. At least I hoped so. With all the snow, the light might not be able to penetrate.

That was the least of my problems. What if Dan wasn't waiting for me at my place? What if he was asleep? What if Casper hadn't understood me? Or she got lost? Or the mug with the note fell off?

Then again, if Dan did get the note and figured out my clue...

I guessed it would take Casper thirty to forty-five minutes to run home. It would take Dan twenty minutes or so to drive out here—if the roads were open.

And if he got the note right away.

Could I last that long? How long could a person last in freezing temperatures with practically no clothes on? I'd never been so cold in all my life.

I searched the front and back seats again, hoping to find a lost sweater tucked into the tuck-and-roll, an old blanket under the seat, anything to wrap up in.

My backpack! I had stuffed the macramé wall-hanging I'd purchased from India. It was better than nothing, I thought, as I grabbed my pack, dumped out the contents, and found the wadded up tie-dyed cloth. I wrapped it around myself, mummy style, slipped the empty backpack over my feet, and lay down on the back seat for added warmth.

And waited.

After trying to stay positive for nearly two hours—and about to give up on anyone finding in time—I thought I saw a light.

Headlights.

A car! A car was coming!

Dan had gotten my clue and—

Another thought reared its ugly head. What if this wasn't Dan? What if this was the killer back to retrieve the money and photos?

I reached over and made sure the doors were locked, even though I'd locked them as soon as Casper had left. Of course, if someone wanted in, they could break a window or stab the canvas convertible top with a knife.

The headlights pulled up in back of my car.

Searching for a weapon in case this wasn't Dan, I spotted the gearshift. Fifty-seven Chevys were made differently from the cars of today. And so were the gearshifts. This one actually unscrewed from the steering wheel. Frantically, I twisted the knob. It came off in my hand. Not what I wanted. I screwed it back on, then twisted the gear stick, removing it from the side of the steering wheel.

Holding the stick in my hand, I raised the knob end like a hammer. And waited.

I watched for sign of an intruder. Out of the corner of my eye, I saw something move by the driver's side.

Someone was wiping away the snow that had collected on the window.

I pulled back, watching for a face to appear.

A familiar face.

I hoped.

The side of a gloved hand pressed against the window. A shadow loomed.

Closer. Closer.

As the shadow pressed itself to the glass, a hideous, deformed face materialized.

A mask! Whoever it was, was wearing a facemask. To protect himself from the cold? Or to obscure his identity?

The hand pounded on the glass. I started and jumped back, nearly dropping the gearshift. I couldn't hear the sound, but I could feel the force rock the Chevy.

He was trying to break the window.

The hand disappeared. Uh-oh. He'd probably figured just pounding with his hand wasn't going to break the window. No doubt he was looking for a rock.

I stared at the window. Suddenly the hand reappeared, pressed against the glass, this time without the glove. Three digits—the thumb, index and baby fingers—were visible; the other two tucked away.

The sign for "I love you."

I reached over and pulled up the button lock. The car door opened.

If the murderer knew sign language, I was in trouble. The masked figure leaned into the car, then pulled off the mask.

I burst into tears. "Dan!"

# 15

"It's okay, Connor. You're going to be okay." Dan removed his jacket and wrapped it around me. He took his flannel shirt off and covered my legs, leaving him with only a thin, long-sleeved T-shirt to keep out the cold. "Sorry about the ski mask. It was so friggin' cold out there. Forgot about it. Didn't mean to scare you."

I was shivering so badly, I nearly shook the jacket and shirt off. My teeth were chattering too much to talk and my fingers were to stiff with cold to sign. I hoped I still had nipples.

"Let's get you to the hospital. You could have frostbite."

Although I hated the thought of going to the hospital, I was too tired to care and too cold to argue. Besides, the thought of devoted nurses wrapping me in heated blankets and feeding me warm broth sounded kind of good.

"How-dog?" I managed to sign, patting my leg for "dog."

"Casper's fine. She's at the diner, enjoying a nice reward—double dog chow. She's quite an amazing animal, you know. You're lucky to have her."

I nodded and teared up thinking about her.

"Lucky to have me, too," Dan added, after moving me to the front seat of his truck. With the heater blowing on me full blast, I began to thaw. He started the engine, then looked at me. "Not every guy would rescue his naked girlfriend and not ask questions."

I managed a smile, then frowned. "Dan," I said, teeth still chattering. "Call...the sheriff."

Dan looked puzzled. "He's still at the hospital. You can talk to him when—"

I shook my head. "No. Sheriff Locke. In Bogus Thunder. There's been another murder."

Dan put the gear in neutral and twisted in his seat to face me. "What are you talking about?"

"Mariposa...in the tree...I found her body. She's..."

"What?"

"I think she's been strangled. It's almost the same M.O. as Zander."

"Somebody hung her?" A look of disbelief distorted his face.

"I don't know. There was a rope around her neck...and marks." I tried to shake away the grisly vision.

Dan pulled out his cell phone. No reception. He slapped it closed and stuck it back in his pocket. "It'll have to wait until we get into town." He shifted into first gear.

I put my hand on his arm. "Wait. There's more."

He put the gear back into neutral.

"In her hand. I think she was holding a token, like the one Zander had."

Dan's lips tightened. He threw the gear into first again, stomped on the gas pedal, and sped out of the sequoia forest, back to civilization, Flat Skunk-style, that is. As he drove, I tucked my legs under me and leaned my head on his shoulder, snuggling next to him for comfort and warmth until we reached Mother Lode Memorial. Now and then I tried to flex my stiff fingers, hoping the feeling in my extremities wasn't permanently gone. The thought of losing even one finger—for a deaf person like me who relies on her hands for communication—terrified me. I balled my hands into fists, which made me think of Mariposa again—how her hands had been tightly fisted.

I flashed on the casino token and shuddered, not from the cold, but the thought that the same person who had murdered Zander most likely had murdered Mariposa.

The key to all this had to lie in those casino tokens.

Turned out I didn't get to stay at the hospital and be waited on hand and foot by a ward full of caring nurses. Instead I was examined from finger to toe in Emergency, treated with an antibiotic, given a tetanus shot, and handed a pair of cotton gloves to help the healing. Apparently I had "pre-tissue skin damage"—in other words, no frostbite, at least not enough to amputate anything, luckily. The doctor promised I would be playing the piano again as soon as I got my hearing back and took lessons.

She also patched up the scrapes I'd incurred from the branches and took X-rays for broken bones that might have resulted from the fall. I was reassured by the medical team that the hair I'd lost from my scalp would, in layman's terms, "grow back," but they could do nothing for my general aches and pains caused by the exertion of tree climbing, other than give me Ibuprofen and a heating pad. They handed me a pair of old scrubs to wear home under Dan's jacket and sent me on my way.

For this, they charged me the equivalent of a month's rent.

Meanwhile, Dan had called Sheriff Peyton Locke in Bogus Thunder and reported to her what I'd said about Mariposa. He'd also gone up to see Sheriff Mercer and fill him in. I had a feeling the sheriff might try to break out of the hospital when he heard the news. And probably blame me.

When I finally exited the emergency room and entered the waiting area, I found Dan sitting in a neon orange chair, reading a tattered copy of *Modern Maturity*.

I grinned when I saw him, relieved he was waiting for me. He stood up, dropped the magazine on the chair seat, and gave me a big hug, careful not to squish my aching body.

He made me feel good enough to tease him. "Any good articles in there?" I nodded toward the magazine.

"The usual. Learned a lot about IBS."

"IBS?"

"Irritable Bowel Syndrome. Do you know it affects—"

I held up a hand. "Never mind. Just take me home before I get IPS—Irritable Patient Syndrome."

"Cute outfit," Dan added, giving me a once over.

I looked down at the baggy, frayed scrubs, topped by Dan's black leather jacket. "You should see what I have on underneath," I said, raising an eyebrow.

"If you're trying to look seductive, you could use a goofy hat."

I touched my head where I'd lost some hair and glared at Dan.

He laughed and we headed for the car.

By interior car light, I talked and signed to Dan as he drove us back to my diner.

"What did Sheriff Locke say?"

"She's calling Deputy Clemens and meeting her at the tree. Also EMTs and Arthurlene, if she can get a hold of her."

"Did you suggest the fire department? They're going to need ladders."

Dan nodded. He glanced at me between trying to keep his eyes on the dark, slick road. "She wanted to know if you touched anything."

"No! I mean, I had to find out if Mariposa was dead...and I needed the blanket she was lying on...and then I had to move her hair...and then there was the rope...and the token..."

"That's what I thought. I told her yes."

"Dan!"

"Look, it doesn't matter. What matters is you're safe, no matter what you had to do to get out of there."

I nodded, appreciating his understanding.

He stole another glance at me. "Later we'll talk about why you were naked when I found you."

By the time Dan's truck reached the diner, I couldn't wait to see Casper. I wanted to shower her with hugs and kisses and show her what a great dog she was. As soon as Dan parked, I leapt out of the car as quickly as my aching body would allow.

"Casper!" I called before Dan got the key in the lock. I knew she'd be waiting for me on the other side of the door, barking and wagging impatiently. Dan unlocked the door and pushed it for me. I was ready for Casper's enthusiastic welcome.

"Cas—"

Her name caught in my throat.

My diner looked like it had been hit by an earthquake.

And there was no sign of my dog.

I started in but Dan pulled me back before I could go in search of Casper.

"Wait here!" he said, pulling out his gun.

"Oh, God! Casper! Dan, where is she—"

Dan waved me to silence and entered the diner. I waited anxiously on the porch, as Dan disappeared into the kitchen. Moments later he reappeared.

No Casper.

He headed for the living area.

No longer able to wait, I stepped inside and took in the mess that had once been my home. Everything, it seemed, had been turned upside-down and inside out. But I didn't care.

All I wanted was to find Casper.

Alive.

Before I could take two steps, Dan reappeared with my dog.

"Casper!" I ran to her, and practically fell to the ground to embrace her. "Casper, oh my sweet baby, sweetheart, sugar, lovey..." Casper licked me, her tail wagging so hard it swung her butt from side to side on the slippery floor. When I finally relaxed my hug, I saw the rope.

Someone had tied a rope around my dog's neck.

Untying it, I looked up at Dan. "Did you tie her up?"

Dan frowned and shook his head.

"Then why—"

"She was tied up in the bathroom when I got there. Barking her head off."

"What—" I dropped the rope and hugged my dog again.

"I also found this." Dan held a sheet of paper by the corner. "It was on the floor next to her."

I reached for the paper but Dan held it high. "Don't touch, just read." I looked at it. Typed on a computer, and printed on a desktop printer—my own?—I read the large bold font.

HEAR NO EVIL. SPEAK NO EVIL. KEEP YOUR MOUTH SHUT, DEAFIE.

I shook my head. "Who would do this? What do they think I know?"

Dan set the paper down carefully, then knelt to pet Casper. "I don't know, Connor, but there's something else."

"More? Isn't this enough?" I shouted.

When I stopped, Dan continued.

"The rope around Casper's neck..."

I nodded. I hadn't really studied it, too eager to get it off my dog.

"It was a hangman's noose."

# 16

After Dan called Deputy Clemens to report the break-in, he and I set about righting my home. Clemens was too busy checking out Mariposa's place to come by and I couldn't wait. Besides, I had a feeling this guy knew enough not to leave fingerprints.

Kitchen cupboards, clothing drawers, and my filing cabinet had all been dumped on the floor. Someone had obviously been looking for something. My notes? I wondered if my office had been hit, too, but I was too tired to deal with that at the moment. It could wait until morning.

It didn't take Dan the Detective long to locate the point of entry. The front door. He'd forgotten to lock it when he rushed off to find me in the sequoia forest. Otherwise, the intruder wouldn't have had a prayer of getting in. After a break-in about a year ago, I'd double-locked every door and even added locks to the windows. This place was a fortress—when you remembered to lock it up.

"Sorry about that," Dan said, shaking his head.

"It's not your fault. You were in a hurry."

"Anything missing?" he asked after we'd put most of the place back together. One good thing about having all your stuff messed up—you end up throwing half of it out when you realize it's not worth cleaning up.

I shrugged. "Aside from my notes, nothing else of real value. At least not that I've noticed yet. My underwear is all there, so that rules out a love-obsessed stalker. And my stash of chocolate—so it obviously wasn't a woman."

Dan nodded as if he'd expected that. We were both certain that whatever was going on, it was tied to Zander. Somehow.

It was after midnight before he and I headed for bed. I let Casper sleep with us as a special treat. The possibility of losing her...that noose around her neck...

As soon as I found out who did this—and I would—I was going to kick that son of a bitch's ass. If I didn't kill him.

I tossed and turned most of the night. The sofa bed was hardly big enough for Dan and me, let alone Casper. I had nightmares about being trapped in an avalanche. With Bigfoot. Naked.

Where was a good pirate dream when I needed it?

By morning, I had bags under my red eyes, my bruised and scraped body ached all over, and even my hair hurt—what was left of it. Instead of my usual jeans and logo T-shirt uniform, I opted for a black velour warm-up suit over long underwear. Dan had slept in, but I accidentally woke him when I dropped my backpack. He rolled over, his arm shading his eyes, just as I was about to head out with Casper.

"Where are you going?" he said, signing, "Where go you?"

"To place a bet. I'm feeling lucky. Your mocha is in the microwave, ready for a reheat whenever you get up."

Dan propped himself up on his elbows. His hair stuck out like a porcupine. He looked adorable. I wanted to pet him.

"Connor. Someone tried to kill you yesterday in that tree, then broke into your house, ransacked it, left you a warning, and could have killed your dog. And you have borderline frostbite. Do you think it's wise to pursue this? Whoever's doing this means business."

I went over and kissed him, then ruffled his spiky hair.

"I feel fine," I lied. "I just want to check out the Gold Strike Casino. Both Zander and Mariposa had tokens in their hands. And there were those hidden pictures of the casino employees cheating the customers. Mariposa knew about it."

"And look what happened to her."

I nodded. "But she was probably blackmailing them—the photos, the money. I think that's what got her killed."

"Yes, and whoever it is knows you were up in her tree snooping around and they probably figured you found the photos. That's why they left that warning. Butt out, Connor."

"Thanks for the advice, Dan," I said coolly and grabbed my backpack. I headed for the door, then turned back. "What about you? Are you just going to stop your investigation? I'm sure the killer knows you and I are..."

"Are what? Friends? Partners? What are we, Connor?"

I twisted the ring on my right hand.

"I'll be back soon. Besides, I'm bringing Casper. She'll take care of me, won't you, girl?" I gave her a pat.

Dan started to say something, but I pretended I didn't notice and headed out the door. Being deaf has its advantages.

The Gold Strike Casino occupied several acres of land surrounded by random volcanic rocks, sparse Manzanita bushes and scrub oak, and California poppy fields. The old Gold Strike Mine, once an active producer of gold, had long since been picked clean and deserted, leaving behind an empty carcass, mounds of tailings, ruined soil, and little vegetation. Although tourists would never know it, the Gold Strike Lake is man-made, just like the wealth brought in by gambling, and the "Gold Strike Mine Ride" for kids is bogus, just like the odds of winning at the casino.

I pulled up in my Chevy, which had been towed back to my diner early in the morning. Luckily I had another set of keys at home—next I'd have a set made to hide in the car. I parked in the expansive lot already filled with cars, trucks, and SUVs at 9:00 a.m.

With Casper at my side, I headed for the front entrance of the main gaming room that was shaped like a giant gold nugget. It was flanked by Hollywood style adobe buildings designed to look like the wild west of fifties television. Neon signs flashed rhythmically, enticing the would-be gamblers to "Strike It Rich!" "Go for the Gold!" "Stake your Claim!" and other promising clichés. The place looked like a mini-Las Vegas, complete with "All You Can Eat $5 Buffet" (with coupon), "Free Drinks!" (non-alcoholic), and "Beautiful Girls!" (no nudity).

Well, not quite Vegas.

A large Indian, at least six feet tall and two-hundred fifty pounds, stood at the door, serving as greeter, I.D. checker, and bouncer. He stopped me as soon as I approached the door and looked down at Casper.

"No dogs," he said simply.

I was ready. It happened all the time. "This is a signal dog. She's allowed in public places, according to public law 94-142." I took a step forward.

He held his hand up.

"You blind?"

I tried to suppress a smile as I looked at his hand. Duh. If I'd been blind, I wouldn't have seen his hand and wouldn't have stopped.

"No, I'm deaf."

"Death?"

"No. *Deaf.* Can't hear." I tapped my ear.

"You can't hear nothing?"

"That's right. Not a thing. Not even your voice."

He frowned at this. I could almost see him process the information.

"How do you know what I'm saying?"

"I read lips pretty well."

He nodded, taking it in. "So why you need a dog?"

"She responds to sound. She alerts me if there are sirens, alarms, loud noises that might mean danger, things like that."

More thinking. "Does she use sign language?"

"Uh, no." It wasn't exactly a lie. She didn't use sign, she responded to it. But I didn't want him to suspect the reason I was there—to spot cheating by sign.

"So, she's not a seeing-eye dog?"

"No, I told you. She's a hearing-ear dog."

He blinked. Wheels turned...slowly.

"Okay, but don't let her pee on the carpet."

I wanted to smack him, but he was bigger than me, and wasn't worth the effort. After years of dealing with the ignorance of some hearing people, I was used to it.

Once we were inside, I wondered if I shouldn't have left Casper in the car. Bringing a dog inside would call attention to me—not something I wanted while snooping around—so I'd have to be cool and keep out of sight.

I headed in, then found myself overwhelmed by dazzling flashing lights, the cloud of second-hand smoke, the sweet smell of fruity drinks mixed with the pungent aroma of the buffet, and all the people who'd been here way too long and had missed way too many showers.

Casper and I made our way through the one-armed bandits that were mostly electronic, although there were a few mechanical. I planned to spend a couple of nickels as part of my cover, but there were few nickel machines—mostly quarters and up. I dug out a quarter, slipped it into a slot machine that featured "The Simpsons," and pressed a button. Homer, Marge, Bart, and the guy who runs the Kwik-E-Mart popped up on the rotating screen. One quarter, gone forever.

I missed the feel of pulling down that slot machine handle. Sort of made me think I had some control over my financial destiny. Pushing an electronic button just wasn't the same. No more gambling for me.

As we made our way to the poker tables, Casper and I garnered lots of weird looks. What? Hadn't these people ever seen a dog before? You'd have thought I'd brought in a rabid skunk the way they stared, pointed, and pulled back. Gamblers needed to get out more.

And then I spotted him. The Yeti. Josh's friend, Brad Edwards. He stood behind a man holding a hand of cards. Brad's arms were crossed over his chest.

I froze, then ducked behind a slot machine, not wanting him to see me. Brad, being deaf, would know that I could tell if he was signing to the dealer. I sat on a stool just out of sight and signed to Casper to sit under the stool. Then I got out my Sidekick and a handful of miscellaneous coins and pretended to feed them into the slot machine.

Scooting my stool over a few inches, I had a fairly clear view of Bradley and my slot machine. I leaned to the side and checked out the dealer—the same one in Mariposa's snapshots. He wore a gold shirt with a black vest that featured the Gold Strike name and logo. His eyes darted around constantly, from the players at his table to what seemed like random glances around the room.

But these were no random glances. He was reading Brad's subtle signs. And beating everyone at the table.

I held up my Sidekick, pretending to enter a message, and snapped a picture with the camera accessory. I took another and another, until I had half a dozen shots of Bradley signaling different hand signs to the dealer. I was about to take another when suddenly everyone around me turned in my direction.

Why were they all staring at me? Had I farted? I looked down to find Casper's head snapping. She was barking! I glanced in the direction of the poker table I'd been spying on and caught Brad's eye. Uh-oh.

"Casper! Hush!" What had she been barking at? I stole another look at the poker table.

Brad was gone.

Someone tapped me on the shoulder. I whirled around and came face to face with a security guard. Apparently he'd already said something to me. "I said, miss, you're going to have to leave."

"But...I told the guy at the front door, this is a working dog. I have a right—"

"I'm sorry, miss, but if you can't keep your dog quiet, you'll still have to leave. You're disturbing the patrons."

I had to think fast. "She's barking because she saw a...rat!"

I could feel the collective gasp from nearby gamblers. The guard glanced nervously around.

"That's ridiculous. We don't have rats at the Gold Strike Casino."

"I'm telling you, she saw a rat, and so did I. Does the health department know about this?"

The guard looked dumbfounded. "I...I'm sure Chief Dakota is in perfect standing with the health department. Now, if you'll—"

A tall man in a gold lame jacket with fringe down the arms and around the hem appeared. I recognized the long black ponytail. Chief Dakota Goldriver.

"What seems to be the trouble, Frank...I mean, Forest Night?"

Frank, AKA "Forest Night"? Did all the employees, Indian or not, use a creative name to appear more authentic? Goldriver included?

"Nothing, Chief. The dog was barking—"

The chief looked me over. "I know you. You're that newspaper lady."

I nodded. "The *Eureka!*. I was thinking of doing a story on the Gold Strike Casino. Thought I'd check out the place."

His piercing dark eyes never left mine. "Perhaps we can discuss it in my office."

I nodded. "Sure."

He gestured for me to lead the way.

To where, I had no idea.

# 17

"Nice place you got here," I said, scanning the office. I'd expected, when I entered, more of the kitschy crap I'd seen in the main casino—Indian artifacts, mining tools, gold veneer, and neon lights.

Instead I found myself in an office the size of my entire diner, decorated simply with a rustic oak desk, a state-of-the-art computer/printer/fax setup, and a well-stocked mini-bar. The rest of the room was taken up with gym equipment. The only unusual piece of "art" was an eight-foot cigar store Indian carved out of redwood. It was kind of like having a lawn jockey at an NAACP meeting. Or that "Hear No Evil" monkey at a Deaf event. Very un-P.C.

Dakota sat down at his desk and fingered a gold token the size of a silver dollar. It was imprinted with a picture of a miner—like the one Zander had when he died. I tried not to let his prestidigitation—now you see it, now you don't—distract me from lip-reading.

"So, you want to do a story on the Gold Strike casino? I'm not surprised. We've had plenty of news coverage. Unfortunately most of it negative. Why would I want you to add to the fire already brewing?"

As a newspaper writer/editor/publisher, I wanted to correct his mixed metaphor, but knew it wouldn't help get what I came for.

"I thought, being deaf, I might see the casino in a different light."

"How's that?" he asked. No sign of the coin.

"Well, I've certainly experienced prejudice in my lifetime. Hearing people think deaf people can't do much. Can't dance. Can't marry. Can't drive. Can't work at most jobs. From the letters I've been getting at the paper recently, it sounds like the Indian nation sometimes has similar problems with prejudice...that ultimately affect the casino."

The coin appeared magically in Dakota's hand. He set it down on the desk.

"What do you want to know?"

I pulled out a pen and my notebook from my backpack, ready to take fake notes. "Well, what kinds of games do you have here besides slot machines?"

He shrugged. "The usual. Pai Gow, Tre Card Poker, Lucky Lady, Seven Card Stud, Texas Hold'Em. We also have bingo, keno, roulette, craps. And for non-gamblers, we have a bowling alley, karaoke bar, hair and nail salon, spa, gift shop, and of course, a food court. We even have a small amusement park for the kiddies."

I nodded and jotted down some chicken scratch as if spellbound by his every word.

"And we're the only ones in the state that offer Dead Man's Hand."

I stopped writing. "Dead Man's Hand?"

Chief Dakota Goldriver turned to the wall behind him, which held a collection of framed yellowed newspaper articles, and took one down. I scanned the rest. Most had headlines like: *GOLD DISCOVERED AT SUTTER'S MILL! GOLD RUSH IS ON!* and other greed-inspiring messages. He set the framed article on his desk and turned it to face me. The headline read: *WILD BILL HICKOK SHOT AT POKER TABLE: DEAD MAN'S HAND.*

Dakota lifted the article and read it to me.

*"At 3:10 on the afternoon of August 12, 1876, Jack McCall shot and killed legendary James Butler "Wild Bill" Hickok while he was playing poker in the Deadwood Saloon. Hickok held*

*what's known as 'Dead Man's Hand' – two pair, black Aces and black Eights – and a fifth unidentified card, suspected of being the Jack of Diamonds, the best possible hand. Unfortunately, after they removed the body, the cards were in such disarray, the identity of the fifth card couldn't be proved.*

--The Doomtown Epitaph"

When he finished, Dakota replaced it on the wall. When he turned back, he was already speaking. "...and that's when Wild Bill Hickok was shot and killed in Saloon Number Ten. Happened in Deadwood, South Dakota, over a card game called Dead Man's Hand."

"Deadwood? Like the TV show?"

Dakota shrugged.

"What was the hand?"

"According to the story, it was two pair—black aces and black eights. No one knows what the fifth card was. But some think it was the nine of diamonds."

"Why would he be murdered over a hand like that?"

"First of all, Hickok was no hero. Reporters like you made up that legend stuff. He came to Deadwood just like the rest of the miners, card players, bunco artists, and outlaws—to get rich. Only he planned to make his money from the miners at the poker tables, not at gunpoint, in spite of the fact that he always wore two pistols on his belt. People say he was good, too. Wore his guns butt forward. Always sat with his back to the wall so no one could creep up and blow his head off."

"If he was so careful, how'd he get shot?"

"He forgot to honor his own rule. He joined a poker game facing away from the saloon's doors. Big mistake."

Dakota flipped the coin over. "A loafer named Jack McCall came up behind him, pulled out a forty-five, and blew Hickok's brains out. Bullet shot out of his cheek and lodged into the hand of a gambler on the other side of the table."

I grimaced and touched my cheek.

"Hickok's poker hand spilled onto the table—pair of black aces, pair of black eights—forever known as Dead Man's Hand. The last card was face down."

"Why did McCall kill him if he wasn't even playing cards?"

"Claimed Hickok killed his brother and got away with it."

"Really."

"But McCall bragged about killing Wild Bill one time too often. He was finally arrested and hung."

Hung.

I felt a chill run up my spine and grabbed my neck.

Dead Man's Hand.

"Wow. Good story. Wish I could put it in my newspaper, but it's already been written up by the *Doomtown Epitaph*, apparently." I glanced at the article on the wall behind him.

"Like I said, we're the only casino out of sixty in the state that offers the game. Only no one gets shot at the end of the hand."

"Or *in* the hand." I smiled weakly. "So how do you play?"

He smiled. "I'll show you some time."

I nodded, then followed up on something he'd said a moment ago.

"I understand there are sixty casinos in California, all run by tribal Indians. According to the Internet, Indian gaming is an eight billion dollar industry."

"Yep. And we're beginning to feel the backlash."

"Like what?"

"Like people claming we're costing them money when we're actually helping the community. They complain about traffic, noise, air and water pollution, increased law enforcement, public safety demands, you name it. They say we're costing the government—your government—hundreds of millions of dollars."

I remembered one letter to the editor I'd received that accused the Indian casinos of costing the government over $130 million a year to cover those expenses. Another wrote that the Indians were supposed to complete a federal environmental impact statement before they could negotiate a gaming compact, which could take years. When the Indian Gaming Regulatory Act was passed by Congress in 1988, it required states to negotiate in "good faith" with Indian tribes.

That was certainly open to interpretation.

"Is any of that true?" I asked.

"Look, we didn't need the 'acres of parking' people thought we would. We've restored the wetlands and native grasses on our two hundred and fifty acre parcel. We didn't build high-rises. But some people don't like the idea of Indians making money."

"And not paying taxes."

"That's not true. Indian gaming in California has returned over a half-billion dollars into local economies. Casino money has helped finance reservation schools, day-care programs, administration buildings, libraries, recreation centers. We even have our own police force. Yes, we also make a lot of money. But seeing as how we've been the poorest culture in America since the White Man took over, don't you think that's fair?"

I didn't know the answer. But that wasn't the question I'd come to ask. Enough of the fake interview. Time for some hard news.

"I also read that one of the CFOs at another casino was arrested and charged with embezzlement, profit skimming, and tax violation. In fact, he was linked to the mafia. Sources said he had three Rolls Royces, houses in three cities and a yacht."

"That's the exception. Most of the casinos are honest. And they've provided well for the Indians. We've gone from poverty and welfare to middle-class lives. And we've helped restore native pride. There's more interest in resurrecting lost traditions and dying languages. I guess you could say that instead of fighting with arrows and rifles, we're fighting for property rights and local control."

"Are all the employees here of Indian ancestry?"

Dakota laughed. "Years ago nobody wanted to be Indian. Now that we're making money, people are going back ten generations trying to prove they're Indian."

"I noticed you have some deaf people working here. Not every employee is Native American?"

He laughed. "No, we're equal opportunity employers. California casinos employ over 15,000 people, mostly non-Indians. Deaf people, such as yourself, have keen eyes and can spot cheaters more easily. They're hard workers, keep to themselves, and are certainly quiet." He laughed at his own joke. "We've had good luck with deafies. And by the way, we prefer the term Indian to Native American."

Deafies? That wasn't a term hearing people used. Only deaf people.

Then I remembered the sign the intruder had left. He had used the word "Deafie."

The hairs on the back of my neck tingled again.

I stood up, suddenly nervous about being alone with this massive man, except for my dog. I noticed he hadn't tried to pet Casper. In fact, he had kept his distance from my dog as he sat well protected behind his large desk.

"Thanks, I think I've got enough to go on. I can't promise when the story will run, but I'll try to keep it fair. Mind if I look around a little on my way out?"

He frowned, then said, "As long as your dog doesn't disturb the patrons. But if she starts barking again, you'll have to take her out."

Her. Most people assumed Casper was a he. Odd. Had Dakota been close enough to Casper to tell she was a female?

"Thanks. I'll be as unobtrusive as possible." I headed for the door, then turned back. "Oh, that game you mentioned. Dead Man's Hand? Which tables have the game? I'd like to check it out."

Dakota picked up the gold token and flipped it through his fingers. "It's a private game. Invitation only. And it requires a special token."

"Like that one?" I nodded toward his hand.

He stopped flipping the coin and tucked it in his pocket.

"Thanks for stopping by, Ms. Westphal."

I headed out to the gaming room and glanced around, hoping to spot Bradley again. He was nowhere in sight. I moved around the tables, observing the players and dealers, looking for familiar if subtle hand movements. I noticed two deaf people dressed in the casino uniform, signing to each other. Stopping to study their conversation, I caught bits and pieces. They were at some distance and obscured by people passing by, so they were difficult to read clearly.

"...what's up with B..." one signed, using a name sign.

"...don't know...disappeared...told me to take over..."

One of the men caught me staring. Most deaf people are used to people gawking at them when they sign, but this one stopped his conversation. I thought he was looking at me, but realized he was looking behind me.

I turned around to see Chief Dakota standing at the door of his office.

Next to him stood Bradley Edwards.

They were both staring at me.

# 18

Next time I go snooping around for information, I'll bring a bull to a china shop, I thought as Casper and I headed for the Chevy. It was sure to draw less attention. What was I thinking, bringing a dog into an undercover operation? Bet James Bond never worked with a dog.

"It's not your fault," I said to Casper, after we got into the car. I scratched behind her ears, along her muzzle, and zigzagged down her back. "That was stupid of me."

And what did it get me other than the attention I didn't want.

Hell. What now?

I pulled out my notes, looked over my list, and crossed off Mariposa. A dead suspect was not a viable suspect. I skimmed down to see who was left; the selection was pretty thin.

The church ladies? Why would they want to murder Zander and then Mariposa? Some kind of religious reason? The deaths did have an air of ceremonial sacrifice. But I couldn't see them climbing up to the roof and hanging Zander. That would have been almost comical.

Bradley Edwards? And Josh? I shook my head. Josh might be radical, passionate, even annoying, but he was no murderer. So what was his connection to Brad, other than old college friends who wanted to establish a DeafTown? I was fairly certain Brad was working with some of the dealers, cheating at the casino—Mariposa had the pictures to prove it. But did that make him a murderer? Perhaps if there was a lot of money involved and he wanted to protect himself.

Dakota Goldriver? Wasn't he making enough money from the casino without having to resort to cheating? Or did he not know what was going on at his casino? He'd have to be blind not to. But would it lead to murder? Maybe for Mariposa, if she was going to expose him. But why Zander? Did he know about the cheating too? I hoped the sheriff had found Mariposa's photographs. Without that proof, there would be nothing to go on.

The last name on the list was the most viable suspect—Kenny-Wayne Johnson. Crazy extremists like him would do anything in the name of "justice." But what would be his motive? He and his group had nothing to do with the casino that I could see. Was it drugs? Or was Zander selling more than a little dope? Arms, perhaps? Where would he get them? And why would he bother, if his drug business was lucrative?

Even though a spouse—or common-law partner—was usually the primary suspect in a murder investigation, I hadn't put India's name on the list—she didn't seem to have a motive. She'd been living quietly with Zander as his partner/lover/"old lady" for years, growing, smoking—and selling—weed. In fact, much more of it than anyone knew. But why kill your partner when you have nothing to gain? And she seemed genuinely distraught when his body was discovered hanging over Wolf's shop.

When I arrived at my office, I hesitated to enter. After my home had been broken into, I suspected the intruder hadn't stopped there, especially if he had wanted more of my notes. I turned the key in the lock, twisted the knob, hoping Casper would bark if anything was amiss.

The door wouldn't budge. Something was blocking it.

The thought of Mariposa's body suddenly loomed.

I pushed with my shoulder and managed to open the door enough to squeeze through.

There was a mess, all right. But not the kind I expected. The floor under the door's mail slot was piled high with letters.

It looked like every single resident of Flat Skunk had written to the *Eureka!*.

I set my backpack down, picked up a handful, and checked the return addresses. Most didn't have any—not unusual. They came from the most prolific writer in town: Anonymous. I tore open a few envelopes and scanned the contents. Vitriol jumped from the pages:

"NO CASINOS in the Gold Country!"

"GET RID of the gambling!"

"Indians—PAY UP!"

On and on they went. A backlash seemed to be forming, not only against the casino, but the Indians who ran it. I wondered what would happen when they found out about the possibility of DeafTown. Would they react as strongly to another minority group buying land, moving in, and siphoning off county finances?

Casper settled on her bed and I settled in my chair. She went to sleep, I went to work. I could have filled the paper with Op-Ed pieces, but didn't have much to write under the headline: *Another Body Found*. Still, I wrote up what I knew about Mariposa's death, after putting in a TTY/TDD call to the M.E. for information on the autopsy.

A little before noon, my office door light flashed. I saved my work, checked to see if Casper was ready to attack the intruder, and headed over to unlock the door.

Dan.

"Why didn't you use your key?" I asked, letting him in.

He looked around my office. "Wasn't sure you'd be alone. Didn't want to barge in on anything."

He was obviously making a reference to the other day when he'd found Josh in my office.

"Well," I said, gesturing to the rest of the letters I still hadn't picked up off the floor, "as you can see, it's just me and my fans."

"Whoa. Secret admirers?"

"Only about half of them. The rest are from crazy people."

"One and the same?"

"Very funny."

Dan sat in Miah's chair, I returned to mine. "What's up?" I asked, flipping my palm up.

"Sheriff Mercer's out of the hospital. He's in a wheelchair and cursing up a storm. Good thing you can't hear."

I laughed. "I'll have to tease him about sitting down on the job. Did you tell him I'm doing the investigating for him? That should get him out of that chair fast."

Dan grinned, paused, then said, "The autopsy on Mariposa came back."

"And?"

"She was strangled."

No shit, Sherlock. "Any drugs involved?"

Dan nodded. "Marijuana. Same as Zander. Sheriff Locke and Deputy Clemens found traces of marijuana at her place."

I sat up. "And the money? The photos?"

Dan shook his head. "Locke said they flipped through all the books, did a thorough search and came up empty."

Great.

That meant the person who'd taken the ladder had replaced it sometime after I left the tree, found the photos and money and disappeared with everything. All before Sheriff Locke arrived.

"Shit."

"Yeah, that was one of the words Sheriff Mercer used."

"Now what?" I spun my chair around, trying to think. All it did was make me dizzy.

"How about lunch?" Dan asked.

We headed for the Nugget, Casper following behind, and took our usual seats at a booth in the middle of the diner. Jilda was on Dan like chocolate powder on a mocha before I could even look at the specials. She poured him a coffee, recommended the "BELT"—bacon, egg, lettuce, tomato sandwich—and took off before I could ask for my usual white trash mocha. Although the Nugget had finally succumbed to the pressure of buying an espresso machine, it had mysteriously broken down a few days after it arrived, and now served as a decoration rather than an appliance. Two glass coffee mugs filled with jellybeans sat on top of the machine, topped with skunk and frog Beanie Babies.

When Jilda returned to take our orders, she brought my mocha.

"Hey Jilda, what's the dirt?" Dan asked, grinning at her like a teenage boy eying a hooker.

"Another dead body," she said, a drawn-on eyebrow arched. "That tree-hugging chick. But I guess you know that."

Dan nodded.

"Where's Junior?" I asked, wondering if she'd had her baby surgically removed from her hip.

"Jackson is with his daddy. Court ordered."

I nodded sympathetically, then gestured with a conspiratorial finger for her to come closer. "Jilda, do you know if Zander sold a lot of dope around here?"

Jilda glanced at the other customers before replying, then scooted in next to Dan and played with the sugar packets as she spoke.

"Okay. But you didn't hear this from me. Yeah, Zander sold the shit big time. He and India were raking it in—the money, I mean. I don't know who was buying. I just know they were selling truckloads. I know she's scared now that Zander is dead. She's worried that whoever killed him is coming back for her."

I looked at Dan. India had a valid point.

"Was Mariposa into drugs too?"

Jilda smirked. "Not dealing, just buying. She seemed to have a wad of cash for the stuff. Maybe the tree-saving business is big money these days. Anyway, I don't think that's what got her killed."

Dan looked at her. "You know why she was killed?"

Jilda shook her head. "No, 'course not. But I do know this—most everyone came to Zander's place to buy the shit. Not Mariposa."

"Then how did she get it?" I asked.

Jilda slid out of the booth, leaned over, and said, "Special delivery." Then she winked at Dan.

# 19

"What was that about?" I asked Dan, eying him.

Dan sat up. "Don't look at me. I have no idea."

"She winked at you!"

"She probably has a twitch or something. Besides, she was referring to Zander."

"Yeah, sure." I sipped my coffee, wondering if she poisoned it. Wouldn't put it past her. Now that she was through with Wolf, it looked like she was going after Dan. Who wouldn't? He was the hottest guy in town.

I twisted the ring on my right hand.

"All right," I conceded. "So you think she meant Zander delivered the drugs to Mariposa personally? Or more?"

"Possibly. Or maybe he was into trees too. We know he liked gardening, so to speak. And she was attractive..."

I frowned. "What do you mean, she was attractive?"

Dan blushed. "I just mean, maybe he was more than a tree-to-tree salesman."

My mouth dropped open. How naïve could I be? If Dan thought Mariposa was cute—and he'd just said as much—then why wouldn't Zander also find her attractive? India, playing the role of Earth Mother for so many years, was beginning to resemble her mentor. Feeding off Mother Nature's bounty, she'd grown rounder and softer, and was showing her age—forty-something? Fifty? Sixty? I wasn't good with guessing people's ages. Fresh, youthful, perky Mariposa embodied the new hippie/Generation X. More Flower Child than Earth Mother.

Maybe Earth Daddy was into starting a new garden.

Okay, I was getting carried away with bad metaphors, but it was beginning to look like something was up between the two of them.

I pounded my coffee, skipped the rest of my BELT, and gathered my backpack.

"Now where are you going?" Dan asked, setting his sandwich down. "You haven't even finished lunch."

I stood up and hoisted the pack on my shoulder. "I have a newspaper to run, remember? And I'm going to have to find some words to put in it if I want to keep the Eureka! in print."

"Connor, stay away from this. Someone's watching you. You've already been warned. Now I'm warning you. Leave it to the sheriffs."

I flashed on an image of Sheriff Mercer rolling after bad guys in his wheelchair and suppressed a smile. "I will. I'm not stupid."

Dan raised an eyebrow.

"What?"

Before I could respond, Jilda was back with her coffee pot ready to fill Dan's every need. I gave him a last "Don't-even-think-about-it" look, and headed out the Nugget Café door with Casper at my side.

We hopped in my Chevy and I drove to India's. I still hadn't had a satisfactory interview with her, and this time I was determined to get it. On the way over I thought about all the comings and goings at her place, the hidden marijuana farm adjacent to their property, and the casino token in Zander's stiff hand. If India wanted to find out who killed Zander as much as I thought she did, she had to supply a few uncomfortable answers.

An SUV—a Sequoia (I was really learning my car models)—was parked in front of the house when I pulled up. No vanity plate. I waited a few minutes to see if this was another in-and-out visit. Sure enough, the door opened and out stepped someone familiar.

Wolf Quick.

The owner of the gold panning shop...breaking parole by buying drugs?

I got out of the car as Wolf headed for his Pathfinder, leaving Casper inside the Chevy to keep watch. I nodded at Wolf, but he looked away as if angry—or embarrassed—to see me. I strained to see inside the SUV as he opened the door. No sign of his baby. Hadn't Jilda said he was supposed to be taking care of Junior?

I headed over and rapped on the passenger side door. The window slid down and I leaned in. "Where's your kid?" I asked, glancing at the seats.

"Jackson's with my mother."

Someone had actually given birth to him? "How's India doing?"

He shrugged. "Fine, I guess. I was just...offering my sympathies, whatever."

That was a big word for a guy like Wolf. I looked at him. His jacket was zipped up around his puffy chest. Nothing unusual there—except Wolf wasn't a puffy guy. Layers of clothing?

Or something hidden inside the jacket?

He caught me staring. The electronic window started up. I jerked my head out before he could strangle me. He backed up, turned, and zoomed away, leaving a frosty stream of exhaust in his wake.

Feeling someone's presence, I turned around and spotted India watching me, a scowl on her face, her dogs snapping at her side. At least there was no gun this time.

I took a breath and moved to the porch. "Hi, India," I said, easing toward her while eying the dogs. "Remember me? Connor Westphal."

She nodded. Her eyes weren't as swollen as the other day, but they were bloodshot. As I got closer, I could smell the pot on her.

"India, I have a problem I wanted to talk to you about."

She said nothing.

"Could I come in for a minute? I'm not here as a reporter."

She stared at me for a few seconds, then swung the door open. Turning her head, she said something to her dogs and they backed up.

I hesitated, hoping this wasn't some kind of trap, then stepped through the doorway, turning to give Casper a last look. India closed the door.

Earth Mother was taking her love of nature too far. The house reeked of marijuana, urine, and dog feces. I scanned the one-room shack for a place to sit and spotted a lumpy yard-sale couch covered with a tie-dyed sheet. I had a feeling some of the yellow circles weren't dye and tried to avoid sitting on them. Wasn't easy.

"Want some tea?" India asked, rustling about in her floor-length denim skirt. She tucked her arms in her oversized sweater—Zander's?—and waited for me to respond.

"Uh, sure. That's sounds great. Should warm me up a bit."

She nodded and moved to a kitchenette filled with more yard-sale appliances—avocado-colored stove/oven, white refrigerator, and a homemade sink with pipes visible underneath. A nicked four-person table sat nearby, cluttered with dirty dishes, logoed coffee mugs, including one stolen from the Nugget Café, and some craft supplies—scissors, glue, hemp rope.

I watched her put the teakettle on and retrieve what looked like day-old—week-old?—bakery goods from a rough-hewn cupboard. She rinsed two mismatched mugs and a plate that was surely crawling with salmonella, dried them with a towel that probably carried cholera, and set them on the table. I smiled, then glanced at the dogs that lay at my feet, monitoring my every move. They probably smelled Casper on me—if they could smell anything else in this odiferous place.

While India poured the tea, I tried to glean something from the décor. Other than a colorful but distorted mural featuring images from *Alice in Wonderland* that had been painted on one wall, there wasn't much. I could tell India wasn't a fan of Martha Stewart. She could use a visit from "Extreme Home Makeover." Then again, she might be better off setting a match to the place.

Odd. What had Zander and India been spending their money on?

Connor. Shut. Up! This woman is grieving. And she's making do with very little. Shame on you.

India brought the tea and set what looked like a plate of petrified chocolate cupcakes on the sofa next to me. She pulled up a kitchen chair, sat back, and took a sip of tea. I followed suit—and nearly choked.

After I recovered as graciously as I could, I asked, "What kind of tea is this?"

"Hemp," she said, then took another sip.

I was drinking tea made from rope? I looked for a place to set the cup down and found nothing. All I could do was hold it.

"The cupcakes are made from hemp, too."

I blinked.

"It's legal, don't worry. Hemp has been around for over five thousand years in China. It's been used as an anti-inflammatory, diuretic, even contains a lot of vitamin E and protein."

I nodded. "Good to know." I eyed the cupcake, then smiled. "India," I began, "the reason I came...is, well, I have a medical condition...associated with deafness. It's called tinnitus. Accompanied by labyrinthitis." I watched her expression as I spoke. Her face was a mask—unemotional and unreadable.

"Someone in town—I won't say who—told me you could help."

"I'm not a doctor."

"No, I know. I...when I was in college years ago, I smoked a little grass—everyone did—and it was really helpful in controlling my dizziness. I didn't realize it at the time, but I'm sure you know...studies have shown that one of the benefits of marijuana is the suppression of nausea and dizziness. Since I've been experiencing dizziness lately, I'd like to try it again and see if it helps."

"Why are you telling me this?"

"The person I spoke with said you might have some I could...buy...for medicinal purposes."

"If you have a medical condition, you should ask your doctor."

"I would, but it's such a hassle. I have to go through all kinds of tests, then I only get a certain allotment, if any. And I have to get it in another county, since this one doesn't recognize marijuana for medical use. You know how it is."

She looked down at her cup like a gypsy reading tealeaves.

"Who gave you my name?"

I shook my head. "I can't reveal my sources, sorry. I hope you understand."

I saw a hint of a smile play at the edges of her mouth. She must have appreciated my dedication to confidentiality.

"I only sell medical marijuana. Understand?"

I nodded.

"But not officially. I'm not licensed."

I nodded again.

"How much you need?"

I thought for a moment. "I...I don't know. What do you recommend?"

"I have no idea. Everyone's different. Try a baggie and see how it goes." She stood up, took my still-full teacup from my hands and set both cups on the scarred table. Facing me, she said, "I'll be right back."

She reached into her cleavage, took a key from a long chain around her neck, and inserted it into a misshapen keyhole painted into the Wonderland mural. A section of the wall opened and India disappeared inside. The wall closed behind her, leaving little evidence of the secret door.

Whoa. How cool.

# 20

While India was gone, I took a quick tour of the one-room home, hoping to find something telling about Zander, before she popped back up through the rabbit hole. Waste of time. Most likely anything of interest would be behind that secret door.

My attention kept returning to the psychedelic mural, a kind of Peter Max meets Andy Warhol interpretation of Wonderland, full of disproportioned doors with giant keyholes, twisted playing cards with croquet mallets, Mad Hatter tea cups and teakettles, and of course a pot-smoking caterpillar haloed by puffs of billowing smoke that shaped words like "Peace," "Love," and "Freedom."

Two figures at the bottom caught my interest. They were caricatures of Zander and India, arms around each other, full frontal a la Adam and Eve in the garden. But while India's image was completely naked, it looked like Zander's penis had been painted over with a familiar yellow-centered white flower. While the rest of the mural had depth and detail, this flowery addition was flat and cartoonish. Obviously not the original artist.

Had India—or Zander—been embarrassed by the graphic depiction of the phallus and painted over it? Why a flower instead of a marijuana leaf?

I didn't have time to ponder it. The invisible mural door reopened and India appeared, holding a baggie. I strained to get a peek inside the room, but it was dark except for the flicker of an eerie green glow.

Computer screen?

I had to get inside that secret room.

"Two hundred," India said, handing me the bag of what looked like Emeril's essence spices. I tried not to look too shocked at the price. I fished in my backpack and pulled out my checkbook.

"Cash."

"Uh, I don't have that much with me." I dug into my wallet and found two twenties. "I'll have to go to the bank for the rest."

She nodded. "I'll trust you for it." She handed over the baggie and I tucked it into my pack.

The drugs took hold immediately and I hadn't even inhaled. I was suddenly transformed from anxious to paranoid. What if I got caught with drugs in my possession? Could I plead stupidity?

India made a move toward the front door.

I stayed where I was. If I wanted to know more about Zander it was now or never. "India, I was wondering, do you think Zander might have been killed because he sold pot? Maybe to the wrong person? A crazy person?"

India shook her head. "We're careful. We only deal with people we know. Been in this business for over twenty years, so we know—he knew—what he was doing."

"I saw Kenny-Wayne Johnson here the other day. You don't think he had some grudge against Zander? He's not the most stable guy on the planet." Uh-oh. Had I just given myself away by mentioning I'd seen Kenny-Wayne?

"Kenny-Wayne is a buffoon. All talk. He and his 'army' are too clouded by pot to do anything violent other than kill a bag of potato chips."

She hadn't noticed my slip, but I wasn't so sure about Kenny's non-violent tendencies under the influence. "Do you sell a lot to him?"

She gave me a "don't go there" look.

Uh-oh. I tried a new approach. "What about those church ladies? Any chance their so-called religion required a sacrifice or something?"

"The Carter gals? Nah. MJ makes you mellow, not mean. Other drugs can make you crazy, for sure, but pot is peaceful. Members of their New Millennium Church just sit around and smoke weed and think they see God. They're harmless."

"So they buy enough for their whole congregation?"

"How do you know all this stuff?" India said, eying me suspiciously. "You been spying on me?"

Shit. "No, of course not. I...passed them on the road yesterday, that's all. Recognized their cars."

She seemed to buy my half truth. I pressed on. "What about Dakota Goldriver? I saw him here, too. What does he use marijuana for?"

"Indians and hallucinogens go way back. They practically discovered the stuff. They just don't grow it anymore, so we supply them."

I frowned. "Zander had a Gold Strike token in his hand when he died. Did he do a lot of gambling at the casino?"

India opened the front door and turned to me. I didn't need to be an expert in reading body language to understand her meaning.

"Well, thank you for your help. Let me know if I can do anything for you."

She paused, then said, "I heard about that tree girl."

I nodded. "Mariposa, yes."

"Her death—there were similarities?"

"Well, she also had a token like Zander's. The sheriff thinks she was strangled. So, yes, I'd say there were similarities."

"You think the same person killed both of them?"

I nodded, surprised she was finally offering to talk. "Either that, or someone tried to copy Zander's murder. Why?"

India pressed her lips together as if she didn't want to let any more words out. Finally she said, "I think Zander knew something about the casino. And so did that girl. I think they were killed over it—whatever it was."

"Zander never said anything to you?"

She shook her head. "No. Once he told me we were going to make a lot of money in the next few months. Get out of this hovel and get us a real house. Stop dealing and worrying about the DEA. Too late now."

"Did you go to the sheriff? He'd—"

She shook her head violently. Wisps of hair fell over her face. No way! I shouldn't have said anything to you. If you print that, he may come after me—"

"I won't. Don't worry. But you should report this to Sheriff Mercer. He can..."

"No! No sheriff. Forget it. Just go. And keep your mouth shut. I won't be safe until they catch this killer. Luckily I have my rifle and my dogs."

I stepped out onto the porch and turned back to face her. "Are you sure you'll be all right? Along out here?"

She frowned, backed up, and closed the door in my face.

Casper greeted me as I opened the car door. I let her out to pee, but before I could get her back in, she took off toward the back of the house. When she didn't come back when I called, I went after her. I found her barking at the rear of the house.

"Casper! Hush!" I signed, trying to calm her, hoping India couldn't hear her. She stopped, her tongue hanging out, panting rapidly. I looked in the direction of her attention, but didn't see anything that would incur such a reaction in her. No hanging bodies, anyway.

There wasn't much in the way of landscaping, just a cement patio the size of a basketball court. No picnic table, outdoor furniture, potted plants. The yard was surrounded by an eight-foot high metal fence. To keep the deer from enjoying the patio?

Casper barked again, moving closer to the fence. I checked for "Danger—Electric Fence" warning signs but didn't see any. Still, I didn't want Casper to find out the hard way if the fence was hot.

"Casper! Come!"

She snapped her jaw a few more times, I yelled a few more times, then she stopped and slinked over to me. I took her by the collar and started to lead her back to the car, then stopped and turned back. Where was the rest of the house? The hidden room? I looked at the patio.

Underneath?

I didn't take any more time to consider it. A back door had opened and inch and I thought I saw the business end of a rifle peeking out.

I was halfway down the road leading away from India's when I passed a black SUV. Traffic seemed to be picking up on this deserted country road. I watched for the model and license plate as it passed by.

A Suburban. "AMER MUT" license plate.

Kenny-Wayne Johnson. Back already to buy more medicinal marijuana? I wondered what ailed him that he'd need so much pot. IBS? Hemorrhoids? Bad breath? Whatever kept him off the streets—and out of the government's hair.

I checked my rearview mirror and saw the SUV disappear around the curve. I was tempted to turn around, but before I could act, I caught a movement in the mirror.

The Suburban. It had done a one-eighty.

And it was coming up behind me. Fast.

"Buckle up, Casper. This is going to be one bumpy ride." I stepped on the gas pedal, urging the Chevy to push the limits of its V8 engine. It lurched forward, knocking Casper off her feet.

"Down, girl!" I signed. She climbed onto the floor and lay down.

I checked my mirror again. The SUV was rapidly gaining. I focused on the road, trying to keep from swerving as my spinning wheels caught slick patches.

The Suburban was right on my bumper.

I couldn't see inside the darkly tinted windows to confirm it was Kenny-Wayne, but who else could it be? Jerk.

The real question was why was he trying to run me off the road?

I hit a pothole and the car jerked violently, causing me to nearly lose control of the steering wheel. Casper watched me from her spot on the floor. I wished I could have said something reassuring, but I was fighting for our lives here.

With one eye on the road and the other on the mirror, I saw the SUV fishtailing side to side on the one-lane road, inches from my bumper. I still had another few miles to go before I'd even be close to civilization.

As I stomped on the gas, I had a cold realization.

I was never going to make it.

Spotting a side dirt road up ahead that led to a house on a hill, I gunned the engine. I'd have a fighting chance if the occupants were home. And if they owned a gun. If I kept going, Casper and I would surely end up in a ditch somewhere.

Just as I reached the turnout, I jerked the steering wheel. The tires hit snow and I lost control of the wheel. The Chevy spun a U-turn, came to rest, and died.

I was facing the road I'd just left.

If the SUV followed me, it would hit me head on. Casper and I would be goners.

I gripped the wheel, unable to move, waiting for the impact.

The Suburban kept going. It drove past me, continuing down the one-lane road I'd just come from.

Stunned, I watched until it disappeared out of sight. The last thing I saw was a hand out the driver's side window.

The bastard sent me a message in sign language.

His middle finger.

# 21

"Casper, you all right?" I grasped my dog's head in my hands and gave her a dry shampoo. She leapt up on the seat and gave me a tongue bath. "We're okay, girl. Just had to deal with a little road rage."

Holding my breath, I put in the key and turned on the ignition. The car started. I let out a sigh, wiped the sweat from my brow with the back of my hand, and drove slowly back to town, hoping my transmission wasn't dragging on the ground.

I pulled up to the Penzance Hotel building, parked, and headed up the stairs, still shaking from the NASCAR driving I'd had to do. Hoping Dan was at his office I knocked, turned the unlocked doorknob, and entered. I found him hunched over his desk reading what looked like photocopied letters.

"Letters from home?" I asked, sitting down opposite him. I set my backpack on the floor and petted Casper. Cujo the cat was nowhere in sight. Too bad. Casper could have used a snack about now. That cat was pure evil.

Dan pulled his gaze from the letter he'd been reading and scrutinized me. "What the hell happened to you?"

I held out my arms and turned them over, searching for signs of my run-in with Kenny-Wayne's SUV. Nothing. "What, do I look that bad?"

"Your face is flushed. Your mascara is running. And your hair looks like it's been abused by a vicious blow drier."

"Thanks. You look sexy, too." Actually, he did.

Dan waited.

"I...had a little car trouble, that's all."

If I told him about my visit to India's and my encounter with Kenny-Wayne, I'd never hear the end of it, deaf or not. I picked up his shiny letter opener to use as a mirror, rubbed the wandering mascara from under my eyes, and changed the subject. "So what's up with the letters? Secret admirer?"

He gave me a knowing look, then began reading the letter he held in his hand.

> *"'My precious flower,*
> *I love your restless soul, your poetic mind, your hungry body. You're everything I was and will be again. You've given me back my lost youth, my suppressed passion, my sexual sword. Soon we'll be together, man and woman, innocence and experience, yin and yang ...' "*

I stopped petting Casper. "S-e-x-u-a-l s-w-o-r-d?" I spelled the words to make sure I'd heard them right.

Dan raised his eyebrows.

I laughed. "Who wrote that flowery drivel?"

Dan set the letter down and lifted up an envelope. Turning it over, he said, "No name or address. No stamp or postmark. I think it was 'tree mail.'"

I picked up the letter and looked at the handwritten scrawl. No circles over the "i"s. No spelling errors. Several references to youth and age.

And a drawing of a white flower with a gray center.

"Dan, did you see the original letter?"

"Yeah, why?"

"What color was the flower?"

He shook his head. "I don't remember."

"White? With a yellow center?"

"Uh, maybe."

I leaned over to his computer and Goggled "white flower with yellow center." Several varieties came up. I recognized one—the same one that was featured on Mariposa's bracelet;

the same one painted over India's mural: "Calochortus invenustus. AKA Mariposa Lily."

So what did I have: Male. Educated. Schmaltzy.

In love with a girl half his age? Dirty old man.

"Where did you get these?"

"Sheriff Locke found them. In Mariposa's tree house."

"Where? I searched the whole place while I was there."

"Did you look under the chamber pot?"

Oh God, the chamber pot. Which I had used.

"Which, by the way, had been used," Dan said.

I blushed all the way to my toes. "Did they…test the contents…?"

Dan nodded. "You need more iron." He smiled wickedly.

Enveloped by a rush of heat, I thought my hair might burst into flames any minute. Remind me never to use a chamber pot again. Ever.

I fanned my face and chest with the letter I still held and quickly changed the subject. "So someone was hot for Mariposa. Any idea who?"

"Sheriff's collecting handwriting samples from everyone who knew Mariposa. Shouldn't be long."

True, but I already had a hunch who'd written those letters. I just didn't know how it all fit together.

I headed for my office, switched on the computer, and looked over my meager notes. I still had the same list of suspects, and only a handful of additional clues. I keyed them in.

*1. Dakota Goldriver*

*a. Cheating at the casino?*

*b. Buying dope from India?*

*Link to Mariposa – Being blackmailed?*

*Link to Zander – Ripped off by drug deal?*

*2. Kenny-Wayne Johnson*

*a. Tried to run me off the road?*

*b. Planning to overthrow the government?*

*Link to Mariposa – Hates pacifist tree-sitters?*

*Link to Zander – Ripped off by drug deal?*

3. *Bradley Edwards*
   a. *Cheating at casino?*
   b. *Connection to Josh?*

   *Link to Mariposa – Blackmail?*
   *Link to Dakota – Drugs?*
4. *Church Ladies?*

   *Link to Dakota - Drugs?*
   *Link to Mariposa?*
5. *Wolf Quick?*

   *Drugs?*

As much as I wanted to, I couldn't see Wolf Quick killing anybody.

6. *Dakota and Mariposa*
   a. *Doing business together? Drugs? Blackmail?*
   b. *Having an affair? Big age difference.*
7. *India?*
   a. *What motive?*

I don't know why I bother with these lists. I never seem to add much new. At least it gave me something to do with my hands.

I thought about India, angry at the casino, fearful she would end up the next victim, but not doing much about it—except keeping her rifle handy and her wolf-dogs nearby.

The door to my office opened, distracting me from my thoughts.

"Hey, Miah," I signed, as my twenty-two year-old assistant entered. He set the skateboard he held under his chair, sat down, and placed a handful of comics on the desk. On top was a collectible *Superman* featuring my idol, Lois Lane on the cover. I read the compelling speech bubble: "*Will Superman save the Doomed Damsel from the Lethal Lex Luthor? Or Has The Man of Steel Lost His Powers – For Good?*"

"Hey," he signed, saluting, then flipped his open hands palm-up. "Whassup?"

I shrugged. "Trying to figure out what to write about the Zander/Mariposa murders. Heard anything around town I might have missed?"

Miah shook his head and turned on his computer. "Send me what you've got."

I transferred the data to his computer and he looked it over.

"You think it's all about drugs?" he signed.

"No clue. But it's the one thing everyone seems to have in common."

"What about that tree girl?"

"Mariposa? She and Zander both had casino tokens. Sheriff Locke found some love letters in her tree house. My guess is they were written by Zander." I told him about the money and photos I'd found.

Miah grinned. "Whoa. Blackmailing, maybe? Dakota?"

"Something like that. Don't know how I can prove it..." I paused. I had an idea. "Miah, I think India has a computer in a hidden room. Do you think you could—"

He didn't let me finish. "Sure. Does she ever leave the house?"

"You can't do it from here?"

"I'm not a magician, boss. If I were that good, I'd be filling my bank account with mob money. No, I'd have to see it. Can you get her out of the house?"

"That's breaking and entering, Miah. I can't let you do that."

"Why not? You do it all the time."

"That's because I'm foolish, as your father often says. Your father, the sheriff, I might add. Besides, then I'd be accused of contributing to the delinquency of a minor."

"First of all, I'm not a minor. Second, I'm already a delinquent. Third, it's not illegal trespass if you have a reason to enter."

"And your reason?"

"I smelled smoke?"

"You're not going to set fire to the place, are you?"

"Of course not. Now, do you think you can get her out of there?"

"I'll think of something. How about tonight?"

Miah gave me a thumbs up. Now all I had to do was come up with a plan to get the reclusive India out of her house for an hour or so. And figure out what to do about the dogs.

I spent the rest of the afternoon Googling names and doing background checks on my suspects. Dakota Goldriver didn't seem to exist. As if by magic, he appeared on the scene about the time the Gold Strike Casino was being proposed. Most likely his name was an alias. I'd have to look at the casino property deed to find out more. Keying in a request for information on the sale of the land for the Gold Strike Casino, I found the name of the tribe—the Martis Indians—an offshoot of the indigenous Miwoks. Another search revealed the band had broken off from the Miwoks after disagreements over plans for the Casino.

Interesting.

Also interesting—I still couldn't find any reference to Chief Dakota Goldriver. According to the document, the head of the Martis band was a man named Duncan Grant. Same initials. He claimed to be one-eighth Indian—which was all it took to head up an Indian casino. But when I did a search for his birth certificate, I found no relatives belonging to any Indian tribes. His heritage appeared to be a mixture of Spanish, Mexican, Creole, and Irish.

When I checked Kenny-Wayne's background, I found a boy who was raised in foster homes, a teen who had quit school in the ninth grade, and a man who was in and out of jail for minor infractions—drunkenness, drugs, theft, vandalism, and assault.

No surprises there.

A search for the church ladies came up empty—except for a connection to a murder twenty years ago in Volcano. Seems Big Ruth and Little Ruth were "questioned" regarding the death of their former pastor, who died mysteriously on a retreat. The pastor, who called herself Queen Mother of The Millennium Ministry, overdosed on 'schrooms, stripped off all her clothes, and dove into Lake Miwok in the middle of the night. Official cause of death was suffocation by drowning.

Bradley Edwards' bio was pretty straightforward. Graduated from Gallaudet University with a degree in business. Son of a wealthy hearing couple who made their money, ironically, producing "talking books"—audiotapes of novels read by semi-professionals. Something their deaf son Bradley would never be able to enjoy. Like Josh, he'd been active in the removal of a hearing president at the University and replacement by a deaf president. He'd also formed a quasi-fraternity, DeafXtreme, a radical club that promoted the use of sign language only—no speech, lip-reading, bi-bi—bilingual and bicultural—or total communication—the use of all forms of communication. The club was disbanded after a group of bi-bi deaf students—bilingual, bicultural—cried "discrimination." Another irony.

No other skeletons in his closet. That I could find, anyway.

Mariposa Sunflower came up when I searched her real name, Staci Morris. She was senior class president at Chico State, belonged to a number of college clubs, including the Horticulture Club, Environmental Club, Earth First Club, and Rainbow Chicks Club.

I waved to Miah to get his attention. "You ever heard of Rainbow Chicks Club?" I signed.

Miah laughed. "Yeah. You thinking of joining?"

"What's so funny?"

He sat back, grinning at me. "You never heard of them?"

"No, that's why I'm asking. Mariposa belonged to a bunch of clubs while she was at college. One of them was the Rainbow Chicks Club. So what is it? Something like Girl Scouts?"

Miah shook his head. "I don't think this group sells cookies or earns badges. Their sign isn't three fingers in the air, either." He made the sign of Girls Scouts.

"What are you talking about?"

"More like this." Miah tapped an "L" on his chin.

My mouth fell open.

"Mariposa was a lesbian?"

# 22

"You seem surprised," Miah signed.

"No. Well, yes. I mean, I thought she was having an affair with Zander. But if she's not into men, then there goes that theory."

"It doesn't necessarily disqualify men. Maybe she's bi—and I'm not talking about deaf bi."

I shrugged, nodded, and shook my head, totally confused. Was I ever going to find a solid piece of evidence in these murders?

I turned to the window, rubbed a circle clear on the foggy glass, and gazed out, trying to put the pieces together. A familiar hulk lumbered toward the Nugget Café.

I stood up and grabbed my jacket and backpack. "I've...gotta go. Meet me here tonight around seven and we'll head over to India's. I've got an idea on how to get her out of the house. Should give us an hour or so. Is that enough?"

"What do you mean 'us'? I don't need a partner."

"I'll stay out of your way. I'll just look around while you work on the computer."

Miah shook his head but didn't argue—at least, not out loud.

"Watch Casper for me, will you? I've been running her around like crazy."

Miah gave me a backhanded wave without looking up from the computer. I blew a kiss to my dog and closed the door behind me.

First stop: The Nugget Café. I needed to see a man about a murder attempt. In a safe, public place.

Kenny-Wayne was sitting in a booth alone when I entered. I squared my shoulders, marched over to his table, then slid in opposite him like he was expecting me.

"Mind if I join you?" I smiled. I didn't bother to remove my jacket.

His eyebrows bunched. "What do you want?" His thin lips, relaxed speech, and wad of food in his mouth didn't make lip-reading easy. What I saw was more like "whu y'wan?"

"I want to know why you tried to run me off the road." I hoped I spoke loudly enough for neighboring diners to hear me. I wanted witnesses, in case I didn't make it out of the Nugget alive.

He laughed. "I wasn't tryin' t'run y'down. I was tryin' t'git ya t'pull over. Y'were takin' up th'whole road and drivin' like a ole lady."

Was this true? Had he just been trying to pass me? Worse: Did I really drive like an old lady? Them's fighting words.

"Then why did you do a one-eighty right after you saw my car?"

"I gotta call on m'cell from m'neighbor sayin' m'ex-wife was tryin' t'break inna m'trailer. Th'bitch wants everythin' I own. I wasn't gonna let 'at happen."

At least, that's what I thought he said.

I was dumbfounded. "Then why didn't you just signal me to get out of the way?"

He slapped the table. "I did! I was layin' on t'horn t'whole time!"

Now I was deaf and dumbfounded. I pointed to my ear. "I'm deaf. You didn't know?"

His eyes widened. "Deaf? That why y'talk 'at way?"

*Yeah, what's your excuse?* I wanted to say. "So you weren't chasing me?"

He scrunched his face. "Hell, no. Why would I wanna do 'at?"

Good question. I had another good question. I lowered my voice—at least I hoped I did. "Kenny-Wayne, do you buy marijuana from Zander and India?"

He blinked three or four times, then glanced around. "Hell, no."

"I saw you at India's yesterday. It looked like you were headed there again today."

He moved the salt and pepper shakers around the table. "So? I...just went out t'pay m'respects. No law agin 'at, is'ere?"

I raised my eyebrows noncommittally. Was there more than drugs involved in their relationship? Any chance Kenny was having an affair with India? Well, he wasn't going to confess anything to me.

"Have any idea why Zander was killed? And Mariposa?"

"Th'tree girl? Nah. Not Zander neither. He's a straight-up guy. India, too."

I tried another approach. "You know, your shotgun shell was found near Zander's body. Can you explain that?"

"Was m'bullet in 'im?"

"No, but—"

"Well, then, I guess that settles that."

Jilda appeared at the table with her baby on her hip. The hip-hugger looked frighteningly like Wolf. Poor thing. Jilda eyed me before asking Kenny-Wayne for his order. I took the opportunity to slide out of the booth.

"Next time y'got someone on yer tail, pull th'hell over," Kenny-Wayne ordered.

"Next time you want to pass someone, try signaling." Remembering the obscene gesture he'd given me, I added, "With your *turn* signal, not your middle finger." I circled my right index finger around the letter "O" of my left hand.

He imitated the sign awkwardly. "Wha's'at mean? 'Blinker' or somethin'?"

"Something like that," I said.

Or something like *asshole*.

It was time to go to church.

Since they were a long shot, I wanted to rule out the Carter couple before I talked with anyone else. I drove to their enclave, which looked more like an expensive spa than a house of worship. A large neon and stained glass sign, shaped like a Bible, greeted visitors, proclaiming the name of the congregation: "New Millinnium Ministry." Unfortunately, the sign-maker had misspelled "Millennium." Guess no one really noticed—or cared—other than a newspaper publisher.

I parked in the large lot next to the Yukon SUV I'd seen the Carters drive to India's place and took in the expansive snow-covered lawn that framed the main building. Designed to look like a royal palace, the "church" was decorated with gilded doves, ornate stained glass, and other pretentious religious symbols. A large fountain, featuring an angel spewing water from its mouth, stood in the center of the front lawn. Reminded me of one I'd seen as a kid—only that one was peeing, not spewing.

I entered through one of two oversized doors that said *Welcome* in blue neon lights. If I thought the outside of the building was breathtaking, the interior nearly made me gasp. The vast space, about the size of a college basketball gym, was encircled by blue velvet-covered chairs. Inside the circle painted on the hardwood floor was an intricate design that looked like a maze. The swirling pattern, a series of concentric circles that linked together and curved around, made me dizzy. I pulled my eyes away and took in the walls. I was surrounded by giant woven panels, each one representing dream-like images of angels frolicking among clouds. Upon closer look, the clouds appeared to emanate from the ground, like giant speech bubbles.

Those weren't clouds of heaven. That was smoke, woven into the scene!

Inside each smoke cloud were catchy self-help phrases: "Know Yourself," "Find Your Purpose," "Be Loved," "Feel Special," and "Make a Difference." The only one missing was "Say No to Drugs."

"Hello?" I called into the empty space.

Moments later Big-Ruth, covered in her blue cape, appeared from behind a door on the left.

"Yes?" she said. "Oh, Ms. Westphal. Come to join our church?"

I smiled. "Uh, it's lovely...all the gold and the angels...and the maze is..."

She nodded proudly. Her sister, Little-Ruth, wearing the same type of blue cape, joined her from the anteroom. "It's cool, isn't it," Little-Ruth said. "We call it 'The Path to Enlightenment.' If you have a problem, you begin over there." She pointed to the outer edge. "Then you walk the path as it weaves back and forth and around and around." She gestured as she spoke, waving her hands back and forth and around and around. "When you end up in the middle, you're enlightened! Your problem is solved."

"Wow, that is cool. I could use one of those in my newspaper office."

Big-Ruth smiled. "Is that why you're here? For a story about the church?"

"Uh, sure. I've been planning to do an article on the New Millennium Church. Soon. But today I'm trying to find out more about the deaths of Zander Nicholas and Mariposa Sunflower. Did you know them?"

"Oh ye—" Little-Ruth started to say, but Big-Ruth interrupted her.

"Well, we didn't actually *know* them. They weren't members of the church. But living in the same area of course we knew *of* them."

I looked at Little-Ruth for confirmation but she said nothing. "I thought I saw you out at India's place yesterday," I said to both of them.

Without letting her pasted-on smile fade, Big-Ruth said, "Yes, we were bringing our condolences to India in her hour of need. We were hoping to get her to join the church. It can be a great comfort at times like this."

I took a breath. I was getting nowhere. Time to amp it up. "Listen, Ruth, I'm not with the police. I'm not here to investigate you. I just want to find out what happened to

Zander and Mariposa. And I understand Zander sold pot to a number of people in the area. Do you think that might have gotten him killed?"

"Why ask us?" Big-Ruth said, still smiling.

"Because I think you bought pot from them—for religious purposes, of course."

Little-Ruth looked down at her shoes and pressed her lips tighter as if to keep from talking. I caught Big-Ruth as she shot her a look, then turned to me. "We may, on occasion, partake of spiritual enhancers, but only to better communicate with God. Just as Christ had wine, we have...weed."

I suppressed a laugh, which wasn't easy. "I...understand. So do you think that's why Zander was killed—because he sold drugs, maybe to the wrong people?"

"We have no idea," Big-Ruth said, speaking for herself and her daughter. I had a feeling she did that often.

"Did you know Mariposa Sunflower, the college girl who was living in that tree?"

This time Little-Ruth shot Big-Ruth a look. I wished I could have read the meaning behind it. "We may have visited her," Big-Ruth said, "on occasion, hoping she would join us too. Her pagan beliefs were...well, blasphemous, to say the least. We wanted to show her the light."

Or light her up. "Was she receptive to your light?"

"Hardly. She thought that tree of hers was God or something."

Little-Ruth finally spoke up. "She was weird. We caught her snooping around here one night after services. She had a camera and was taking all these pictures."

"Hush!" Big-Ruth snapped, her smile finally gone. "That has nothing to do with Mariposa's unfortunate demise."

"Why would she want to snoop around here?" I asked.

Little-Ruth said nothing. Big-Ruth shrugged.

"Did she know about the death of your previous minister?" I said it on a whim, hoping to get a rise.

Little-Ruth turned bright red. Big-Ruth's eyes widened. I didn't need a lie detector to tell me I was onto something.

"I don't know what you're talking about," Big-Ruth said.

"I read somewhere that the minister of the original Millennium Church died—drowned—ten years ago. That's about the time you took over the congregation, isn't it? Changed the name to the New Millennium Church? And really started recruiting? Looks like you've spent quite a lot of tithing on the property." I glanced around.

"That has nothing to do with this. Our members give freely to support the church. And the death of Sister Constance was an accident, a tragedy. We're just trying to carry on her work, and ours."

"Did Mariposa know about her death?"

"How would I know?" Big-Ruth said.

"Did you ever give her money for...anything?" The word "blackmail" was such an ugly term.

The smile returned to Big-Ruth's face. "No. Now I must get back to my duties. Please join us on Sunday. We'd love to have you as a member of the church."

With that, Big-Ruth spiraled around, swinging her long cloak dramatically, and exited into the anteroom. Little-Ruth gave me a last look, then followed her sister behind the door. It was a look I couldn't interpret.

As I got in my car, I gazed at the sumptuous snow-covered spread known as the New Millennium Church and had one question.

Where had they gotten the money for such an extravagance? The collection plate?

Or drug sales to their flock?

# 23

I returned to my office to check on Miah and Casper. Miah was playing "Halo" on the computer, and Casper was playing "chase the squirrel" in her sleep. Some watch dog. She didn't even wake up when I entered. Come to think of it, Miah didn't look up either.

"Burglars could walk right in here any time and the two of you wouldn't even notice!" I said, dropping my backpack on my desk and unzipping my jacket. Casper sat up; Miah said something I couldn't read. He paused the game, swung around, and signed, "You mean *robbers*, not *burglars*. Burglars steal stuff when you're not around. Robbers do it when you are."

"Whatever, Mr. Junior Police Officer. Any news?"

"Just this." He handed me an envelope. My name was scrawled on the front. No postage.

"Who brought this?" I asked, tearing open the envelope.

Miah crossed his arms over his chest and waited for me to read the note inside. I did.

*"Hey, Con. Sorry I missed you. Can you meet me out at DeafTown, (formerly China Camp) when you get in? Got something to show you.*

*Love, Josh."*

Love, Josh?

I looked at the note again. He'd drawn a tiny hand by his name, with the thumb, index, and baby finger extended—the ubiquitous "I love you" sign. Even hearing people knew this one.

"When did he come by?"

Miah looked at his sports watch. "Half an hour ago?"

"Did he say anything?"

"Nope. Just asked where you were, then wrote this note and left."

I frowned. Damn. I didn't need this. I checked my own watch, then picked up my backpack and called to Casper. "All right, I'll be back in an hour. Hold the fort for me, will you?"

Miah nodded, glancing at his computer game, currently holding well.

"And if Dan stops by..." I looked at him.

Miah zipped his lip.

"That's not necessary. Just tell him...I'll be back soon." To Casper, I said, "Come on, girl. Let's go."

The drive to China Camp, AKA DeafTown, took thirty minutes, only because I drove slowly over the slick road. The deserted town looked eerie as I drove past a stone marker that signaled the entrance to the main road. Not much was left of the place. A couple of distressed wooden buildings topped with snow that looked like they would collapse under the weight any minute. The main dirt road, a slushy mess, was flanked by wooden sidewalks that may or may not have seen better days. The names of the shops were peeling and faded: *Tong's Mercantile Shop*, *Woo's Gaming Parlor*, and *The Chinese School*.

The place looked forsaken, as expected with a ghost town. I honked the horn, then remembered I wasn't here to meet a hearing person. Josh would never hear the horn.

To my surprise, Susie appeared at the door to the Chinese School.

She'd heard me! I'd forgotten about her cochlear implant.

I waved and got out of the car as she ran to meet me. "Hi, Susie," I signed, then gave her a hug as she rushed into my arms. "What are you doing here?"

"Playing school," she said. "Daddy said I could be the teacher."

"Where is your dad?"

"He's building a town." She pointed to the building she'd just come from. "DeafTown. It's only for Deaf people."

"Yes, I know. Will you take me to your dad?" I signed and said aloud. She held my hand and led me inside the building. We walked past half a dozen old-fashioned school desks that were bolted to the floor. Probably the only reason they were still there. Not much else was, thanks to tourists, looters, and bored delinquents. The walls inside were sprayed with graffiti, the floors covered with litter. I spotted Josh in the back, sweeping—a job that seemed equal to panning for gold in a swimming pool. Hopeless.

"Connor!" Josh used my name sign when he saw me. He leaned the broom in the corner and greeted me with a hug. "So glad you came! Susie, look who's here!"

"I know," Susie signed. She gave me another hug, then headed back to one of the school desks to color the picture she had started.

I looked around the decaying room, then back at Josh, puzzled. "What are you doing? Sweeping? That's how you're going to get your DeafTown built?"

Josh laughed. "No, I'm just cleaning it out for Susie. The place is filthy and I don't want her playing in here with all this mess."

"I wouldn't want her playing in here no matter what. The building looks like it's going to cave in like an unstable mine any minute."

He knocked on a nearby wall. "It's structurally sound, believe it or not. But it won't be for long. Workers are coming in a few days to knock it all down. We start construction next week."

"Great," I signed, trying to hide the fact that I still wasn't convinced this was really going to happen. "So, what did you want to show me?"

Josh took my hand. I let him, but didn't return his tight grip. He waved to Susie to join us, then led me out the back door.

I stood staring at a Winnebago.

I turned to Josh and raised my eyebrows. "What's this? DeafTown City Hall?"

"Very funny. Come inside."

He led me to the trailer and opened the door. Susie leaped inside. I followed her; Josh brought up the rear. Casper decided to stay outside and guard the place.

The inside of the trailer was small and cramped but neat and clean. Susie's drawings were taped up on every free space. She had the upper bunk—her pink spread with piled with stuffed animals, Barbies, and ruffled pink pillows. Josh slept underneath. His was covered with a plain blue bedspread, neatly made.

"Nice," I signed, swiping my right hand over my left hand. "You live here now?"

Josh nodded. "But this is what I wanted you to see." He gestured toward the tiny dining table. A blueprint labeled "DeafTown" was spread open on top.

"So these are the plans?" I said, glancing at them. "I'm not much good at reading blueprints—"

Josh pulled another large sheet of paper from under the blueprint. It was an artist's rendering of the proposed town. I scanned the cluster of townhouses, a small shopping center, a park and community center building with a swimming pool, and a schoolhouse. The design was modern, esthetically pleasing, and impressive. A Deaf Utopia.

"What do you think?" Josh said, grinning proudly.

"Amazing. I...I didn't think it would be this...nice. Although there's no reason why not. You're a very...visionary person."

"We'll have state-of-the-art equipment for Deaf living. Each place will be equipped with signal lights for the doors, phone, everything! Thanks to Brad and his father, this dream is actually going to come true."

I looked up from the drawing. "Josh, what do you really know about Brad?"

"I went to school with him. Didn't see him for years until we reconnected via the Internet. We were both on the

DeafReform chat room. That's where we started talking about DeafTown."

"Does he have a drug problem?"

"What?"

"Drugs. Does he smoke pot or use any drugs?"

"I don't know. Why do you ask?"

"What about a gambling problem?"

Connor, where are all these questions coming from? Brad's cool. He's dedicated to DeafTown. And his father is funding us. I don't want to rock the boat now that this is within our grasp."

"Have you met his father?"

"No, but I don't think—"

"I Googled him, Josh. According to a story in the *Wall Street Journal* he made a lot of money years ago when audio books first came out. That part is true. But he lost it all investing in the dot com boom. He was left with essentially nothing."

Josh frowned. "I don't understand."

"I don't think Brad is using his father's money."

"But he's already written several checks. Good checks."

"So where did he get the money?" I asked.

"Uh ... maybe his father set up a fund for him ..."

"I don't think so. Josh, I think your friend is making money at the casino. A lot of money."

"Gambling?" Josh looked as if I'd slandered his own brother.

I shook my head. "Cheating."

Josh sat down at the small table. I slid in across from him, and told him what I'd learned investigating Mariposa.

"I don't believe it, Connor. He wants DeafTown as much as I do. Maybe more."

"I don't doubt that. I just question how he's getting the money."

Josh shook his head. "I think you're wrong. And if you think he's connected to those deaths, well, there's no way Brad could be involved. He's been great to Susie. He loves Deaf Culture. And the Indians. He's even learned Indian Sign and they're learning ASL. Besides, he was a good friend of

Zander's. He's not a killer. In fact, he hates anything to do with killing. Like those survivalist whackos."

"Hates them?"

"You know what I mean."

"Did he know Mariposa?"

"The girl that got killed? He never said anything about her."

"Well, I'm just telling you what I know. Keep an eye on him and see if you can find out where he gets his money. For me?"

Josh looked down at his DeafTown drawing and nodded. After a moment, he met my eyes. "Speaking of you..." Josh took my hand. "Connor, I haven't forgotten everything you've done for me. After all these years my feelings toward you haven't changed. Now that Gail...I mean, now that Susie and I are alone...Connor..."

And then Josh did something that stunned me.

He got down on one knee.

And so did little Susie.

"Connor," Josh signed, using my name sign.

Susie aped him, also signing my name.

As if they had practiced, together they signed, "Will you marry us?"

I looked at Josh, then at Susie. Before I could say anything, my Sidekick started vibrating in my pocket. I pulled it out slowly and read the message. It was from Dan.

"C. India's place on fire. Where R U?"

# 24

"Fire!" I signed to Josh, holding my fingers up and wiggling them like flickering flames. In spite of the cold I felt a chill run down my back.

Josh got up and lifted Susie in his arms. "Where?"

"India's. I have to get over there. Sorry."

I stepped out of the trailer and ran for my car. Casper stopped playing in the snow and followed me. She leaped into the driver's side, sopping the leatherette seats with wet paw prints. I hopped in after her and started the car.

As soon as I was on the road, I sent a message to Dan on my Sidekick. "Nt thr bt on my way. U?"

I drove on, checking periodically for a response. Nothing. Dan was probably too busy to answer. I stepped on the gas and focused on the slick roads. It wasn't long before I smelled smoke. When I turned up Poker Flat Road toward India's, I spotted the billowing clouds. I thought I might hear the high-squeal of sirens, but didn't.

Following the smoke, I quickly figured out it wasn't coming from India's house. The smoke was coming from the marijuana greenhouse.

I rolled down the window and inhaled, taking in the sweet smell of pot mixed with the acrid odor of smoke. Whoa. Were the deer and the antelope going to play today!

My eyes burned. I rolled the window back up and slowed as I spotted the fire chief's car, the sheriff's car, and Dan's truck on the side of the road. Two fire engines were parked in the snow near the stone wall. I pulled over, decided against cracking the windows to keep the smoke from coming in, and told Casper to stay.

The fire was nearly out, hence the billowing clouds of smoke I had noticed on the way. Unable to see the extent of the damage over the high stone wall, I hopped onto the hood of a fire engine.

The former pothouse was a blackened mess of melted fiberglass, singed lamps, and burnt weed. I choked on the toxic smoke and covered my mouth with my jacket sleeve.

Someone waved to me from the ground.

Dan.

I waved back and hopped down from the truck. Into his arms.

"Are you okay?" he signed, looking me over.

I coughed and nodded my hand, the sign for "Yes." "I was at...an interview." I didn't want to mention I'd been at Josh's place. Dan would start asking questions, and I didn't want to go there. "I got your message and came right over."

"I'm glad you're okay. I thought maybe you were here and someone..." He didn't finish his thought. I squeezed his hand.

I spotted Sheriff Mercer hobbling toward us on crutches. He didn't look happy.

I started explaining before he could accuse me of anything. "Sheriff, I know what you're going to say, but I was nowhere near here when the fire began, I swear."

But the sheriff only nodded. "I know, I know. I saw you pull up."

"You're out of the wheelchair!" I said, surprised at his new form of mobility.

"I couldn't stand it any longer, sitting on my fat ass all day. Doc said I could try crutches if I didn't stay on them for too long."

He adjusted the crutches several times under his arms, looking miserable. But at least he was ambulatory.

"You know what this is?" the sheriff asked, pointing to the smoke-filled area behind him with one crutch.

I tried to look innocent when I said, "A marijuana farm?"

"Any idea whose?"

"Nope, although I could guess, since it's so close to Zander and India's property."

Sheriff Mercer nodded. "Any idea who did this?"

I shook my head. "No, but I think someone may be out to get India. Has anyone checked her place?"

The sheriff frowned, then pulled a cell phone from his pocket.

"Doesn't work out here," I said. "You'll have to use your squad car mobile phone."

Sheriff Mercer shouted at Deputy Marca Clemens who was standing on a ladder, gazing over the stone. I couldn't read what the sheriff said, but I guessed he told her to check out India's place.

When he turned back to me he said, "What makes you think someone's after India?"

"I went by there this morning to talk to her and she seemed to think whoever killed Zander may want her dead, too."

"What reason did she give you?"

"None, really. But I think it has something to do with their pot business. Apparently Zander sold a lot more than just for personal use. Maybe he sold to the wrong people and it caught up with him." I thought about Dakota at the casino, Mariposa's incriminating photos, and Zander's frequent visits to the tree house. Somehow it was all tied in. And it was all about money.

When I saw Deputy Clemens get into the squad car, I turned to Dan and the sheriff. "I'm going with her. I want to see if India's all right."

"C.W...." the sheriff started.

"India knows me, Sheriff. Maybe I can help. Or at least find out who did this."

Before Sheriff Mercer or Dan could argue further, I turned away, reached into my car for my backpack, and followed the deputy to the squad car. That way I didn't have to pretend I didn't hear them.

"Watch Casper for me!" I called, as we headed off.

Deputy Clemens said little as we drove up in front of the porch, then turned to face me. "So the sheriff said you could help, huh?"

I signed "sort of," but said aloud, "Yeah."

"Do you know her pretty well?" Marca asked.

"Sort of" I signed, but said aloud, "Yeah."

"That might help, if she's hysterical or anything."

I followed the deputy up the porch steps and waited while she knocked on the door.

No answer.

"Do you hear dogs barking?" I asked.

She nodded. "And they don't sound friendly." She knocked again.

Nothing.

"India Nicholas? It's Deputy Clemens!" she called, rapping vigorously.

I tried the doorknob. Locked.

The deputy gave me a stinging look.

"What?" I said. "She might be hurt inside. We have to get in there."

The deputy thought a minute, then said, "Wait here. I'll go around back."

I nodded, fairly certain she wouldn't find a way in through that fence. I was right. Moments later she returned, trying to look official while obviously totally puzzled.

"The window?" I suggested, nodding to one of two windows at the front of the house. They were closed and covered by what looked like hemp woven curtains.

"Not without a court order or a justifiable reason to enter without permission."

"But—"

"I better get Sheriff Mercer. He'll want to handle this."

I sighed as I watched her head for the squad car. Apparently the sheriff couldn't drive, so she was acting as deputy/chauffeur.

"You coming?" she asked as she opened the driver's side door.

I shook my head and grabbed my backpack. "I'll stay here. In case."

She gave me a long look, then got in the car and drove off. Good thing I wasn't a sheriff's deputy. Lawful or not, I would find a way inside this house.

I studied the window, looking for a crack, and knocked on the glass. It wasn't glass. Plexiglas. No way to break the pane. I checked the other window. Same thing.

I wiggled the doorknob. It held tight. I remembered all the bolts and locks on the inside. Front and back, the place was nearly a fortress. There was no way Miah could get in to look at her computer unless I managed to get in and leave something unlocked.

I moved to the back of the house and studied the fence. Electric?

Only one way to tell. I'd have to touch it.

Surely it wouldn't be hot enough to barbeque her own dogs?

Or me?

Gathering my courage, I moved in. Using the back of my hand—my ringless hand—I brush it quickly against the fence.

"Yeeouch!" I pulled my hand back, feeling a tingle all over. And not a Dan Smith-type tingle, either. I hoped I hadn't wet myself or anything.

Definitely hot.

I gave the fence a dirty look, then something caught my eye. A patch of dirt under a three-foot section of fence had been dug away, leaving a gap about two feet deep.

The dogs? Had they figured out a way to dig out from under their fenced yard?

I looked at the house again and focused on a backdoor, no doubt doubly bolted and secure. At the bottom of the door was a small square, about the size of a medium-sized pizza box.

A doggy door.

For hundred-pound wolfdogs.

I glanced back at the dugout pit, then back to the doggy door.

It just might work.

Removing my thick jacket and Uggs, I sat on the snowy ground and studied the pit. If I sucked in my stomach and my ass, I might just make it through without getting electrocuted. Then again, I might not.

I set down my backpack, dug through until I found a box of Casper's doggy treats, and stuck a handful in my pocket.

I lay on my stomach, the snowy ground chilling me to the bone. Ducking my head, I pushed myself forward under the fence a few inches at a time. By taking in shallow breaths and visualizing myself a size six, I slithered forward. The toughest part was arching my back—the thought of what waited inches above me gave me a chill—but I kept going, breathing a sigh of relief when my butt was on the inside of the fenced yard. I pulled my legs up—too quickly—scraping my foot against the fence for a split second.

Zap!

It felt like I'd been attacked by a hot vibrator.

I looked at my foot and noticed the hole in my sock. Great. I gave the fence another dirty look and headed to my next challenge.

The doggy door.

Piece of cake compared to the electric tunnel.

# 25

I checked my watch. Deputy Clemens would be back with Sheriff Mercer in ten minutes, give or take. I didn't have much time.

Back on my stomach again, I pushed open the door and peered in. Four wolf-dogs stood facing the door, their heads snapping violently.

Oh God.

"Nice doggies!" I said weakly. I threw a handful of treats as far as I could. The dogs scrambled after them.

And inhaled them.

What now?

I remembered India had used a command on her dogs. Something like "pa-lay" or "ba-lay." It was all I had left.

"Pa-lay!" I shouted. "Pa-lay!"

The dogs stopped barking and lay on the floor.

Oh my goodness. The power of words. Even when I didn't know what I was saying.

I squirmed and wiggled inside, feeling like a fat worm entering a cage of hungry birds. As long as I didn't run out of dog treats I'd be okay.

I hoped.

I stood up, brushed off the dog hair and dirt, and took a quick look around the small room. Spotting something shiny, I headed over and bent down.

A large butcher knife.

Lying on the floor.

With blood on it.

A chill ran up my back.

No sign of India.

My eyes shot to the invisible door. Only it wasn't so invisible. There was a bloody handprint on the painted lock. I plodded over, a sense of dread sweeping over me.

The door was slightly ajar.

Not wanting to taint a possible crime scene, I glanced around for something to open the door further. Before I could reach for a kitchen utensil, the dogs were back.

Snapping and sneering and drooling.

I poured out another handful of treats and threw them across the room. That would only give me a few more seconds. Grabbing a nearby wooden spoon from the sink, I pushed open the door.

Darkness.

I searched for a light switch on the wall but couldn't find one. I stepped in, trying not to touch anything—more than I had to. There had to be a switch somewhere.

I started to take another step and I felt something hit my back.

Stumbling, I tried to regain my balance—and fell down a flight of stairs.

Into darkness.

I wasn't sure I was awake. My eyes felt like they were open, but I couldn't see anything. Pain seemed to be everywhere—my head, my back, my arms, my legs. Slowly I realized where I was.

India's secret room.

Lying on my side, I tried to sit up but couldn't. And then I knew why.

My arms were bound behind my back and my legs tied at the ankles.

Panic shot through me, worsening the pain.

I lifted my head and felt a tightness around my neck.

Oh God.

I straightened my legs—my feet hit something solid. It moved.

"India?" I said.

If she responded, I couldn't hear her. I tapped the object with my feet. It moved again.

Feeling panic rise, I twisted around and rolled in to a sitting position and scooted as far away from it as possible.

Moments later I felt something touch my arm.

Fur.

"Casper?" I called. "Oh God, Casper?"

The fur moved.

And bit my hand.

"Ouch!" I screamed, recoiling.

This wasn't Casper.

India's wolf-dogs! Were they down here with me? Were they tied up too?

Or were they hungrily circling me?

I rubbed my fingers together and felt blood.

Oh God! I had to get out of here!

Leaning forward and tucking my legs underneath me, I stood up, wobbling precariously.

Unable to walk with my ankles bound, I hopped forward. Carefully. I didn't want to stomp on any paws. And slammed into the edge of what I guessed was a table, throwing me off balance.

I leaned forward to steady myself, then hopped in a tiny circle until my back was to the table and my butt hit the edge. I leaned backwards, my bound hands straining, and tried to feel for whatever might be on the table.

My fingers touched something cold and hard.

And familiar.

A computer! This was the source of that eerie green glow that had come from the hidden room. Arching back farther, my hands explored the monitor until I found what I was looking for.

I pressed the button. Nothing. I pressed another.

The screen lit up, casting its glow throughout the room.

I looked around my basement prison. The four wolf-dogs stood at attention, obviously barking their heads off at me. They appeared ready to attack at any moment.

"Pa-lay!" I commanded. "Pa-lay!" The dogs stopped barking and settled onto the cement floor. They still looked menacing, but didn't seem to want to eat me at the moment.

I took a second to scan the rest of the room in case I need a weapon to protect myself. Aside from the computer, the place was empty. No weapons. No drugs. No stacks of money. No India. Just a cement room.

How long had I been here? Long enough to be tied up. I looked down at my chest and saw a rope dangling around my neck. Had someone been about to...hang me?

And was he still here?

Deputy Clemens! Sheriff Mercer! Where were they? Had they come and gone, not knowing I was still here?

*No, don't think that way, Connor.* They're either on their way or they're here. Maybe upstairs, in the house, at this very moment.

They wouldn't leave without me.

Would they?

Noise! I had to make some noise! I might not be able to hear them, but if they were here, maybe they could hear me.

"Sheriff! Help! I'm in the basement!" I screamed. I screamed until my throat hurt. And then some.

No light. No sheriff. Nothing. Was the place soundproof?

I looked for something to throw against the ceiling. That was my best chance of being heard. Besides the computer, there was nothing. And even if I found something, I didn't think I had enough range of motion or leverage to throw it to the ceiling.

I hopped around and looked at the computer.

If the screen was still connected, maybe the computer itself was still hooked up. I scanned the keyboard to get my bearings and leaned over. With my chin, I hit a key. The screensaver morphed into a display of icons. I spotted the cursor, put my chin on the touch pad, and moved it to the Internet icon.

I lifted my head and checked. "Yes!" I tapped the touch pad twice, making the connection. After tedious, painstaking, and sometimes painful, chin movements, I was online with the sheriff's dispatcher, via Yahoo. I chinned in a message: "HLP STUCK INDIA BASMNT CW." I tapped Return.

I sat down on the cement floor and waited while the four dogs watched me like I was puppy chow.

Then I smelled smoke.

I didn't know where the smoke was coming from exactly, but I knew it wasn't left over from the marijuana farm fire. This smoke was close. And it didn't smell like pot. Wood?

Upstairs?

I screamed my lungs out, praying someone would hear me. By the looks of their barking heads, the dogs joined me.

Abruptly, the computer monitor light went out.

I was plunged into darkness again.

The fire?

I lay on the floor, trying to avoid the smoke that seeped into the room. Was it getting hot in here? I started to cough.

Just as suddenly, the room lit up with a shaft of light from above.

Heaven?

Through the smoky haze I saw someone bolt down the staircase.

Dan.

Behind him were Deputy Clemens, two firemen...and Casper.

From the backseat of the squad car, rope-free, I looked back at Zander and India's home and inhaled the fresh cold air. The firefighters had arrived in time to save most of the structure before it was enveloped in flames. One side of the house was charred, but according to Dan, the inside was essentially intact.

"Any sign of India?" I asked Dan, hugging an insulated blanket around me.

Dan shook his head. "But we did find the knife."

The bloodstained knife.

"What about the dogs? Are they okay?" As much as I didn't care for India's dogs, I didn't want them dead.

Dan nodded. "They're in the fenced backyard. Sheriff called animal control. They'll be here soon."

The sheriff limped over on his crutches. "You okay, C.W.?" he asked.

I nodded.

"So what happened here?"

"I ...I..."

"You broke in, didn't you?"

"Not exactly. I...went in through the doggy door. I was worried about India."

"And you couldn't wait for me and the deputy?"

"I...I'm sorry. I messed up." I tried to look contrite.

"Big time, Westphal. I'm so mad I could..." he didn't finish his sentence. Instead, he jammed one of his crutches into the snow, then spun around and limped back to the house.

I turned to Dan and pled my case. "I was worried! She didn't answer the door when Deputy Clemens knocked. I knew she was scared for her life! She thought she was going to be next. And now...it's happened!"

Dan put an arm around me.

"You don't know that. She may have gotten away."

"But the blood. On the knife. On the wall..."

"But there's no body, Connor. If she's still alive, she may be hiding somewhere. Somewhere safe."

I nodded, not convinced. "But don't forget—whoever it was tried to kill me too. Maybe I didn't fall down those stairs. Maybe he pushed me, then tied me up in that hidden basement and shut me in with those vicious dogs. And then he set fire to the house!"

Dan hugged me tighter. "We'll get him. And we'll find India. In the meantime, you're going to go home, lock your doors, and stay there. Understand?"

I nodded. Dan leaned over and kissed me.

Tears sprang to my eyes.

# 26

Dan followed me back to my diner, walked me in and made sure there were no surprises waiting for me.

"Lock up," he ordered, giving me a kiss at the door. "I'll be back in an hour or two. I want to see what comes out of Zander's computer. Arthurlene's got one of her hackers going over it. You going to be okay?"

I nodded. I wasn't worried about someone breaking into my diner. I had my vicious watchdog Casper, enough locks to start a locksmithing business, and my Sidekick, TDD, and some sample communication gizmos for the Deaf in case of an emergency.

"Let me know what you find out. I have a feeling the answers are in that computer. He probably kept his drug business records—and maybe even the blackmail stuff."

"I will. Now, don't answer the door to anyone you don't know. Use your peephole—that's what it's for. I realize this is a small town and nobody locks their doors around here. But this is different."

"I know, I know. I'm not stupid. Just...hurry back."

Dan gave me a kiss and I returned it, not wanting to let go. "I'll be back soon," he said and headed out. I secured all three locks as soon as he left.

Then my eyes fell on the cell phone I'd borrowed from Dan.

The camera.

I sat down at my home computer, transferred the photos I'd taken surreptitiously at the Gold Strike Casino, and printed them out. I had half a dozen clear shots of Bradley Edwards.

And his cheating hands.

"Casper! Come on!"

Stuffing the copies in my backpack, I headed out the door, locking up my diner securely behind me. I still didn't want any surprises waiting for me—and this time I wouldn't have Dan to check for me.

There was only one way to get rid of my list of suspects without killing them all. Find out if they were guilty. Since Dakota Goldriver was at the top of my list, I headed for the casino: "Open All Night!" "We Never Close!"

This time I left Casper in the car to avoid another scene. I had no trouble getting in without a dog, and made my way directly for Dakota's office. A security guard held up his hand at the door.

"No admittance, sorry."

"I...have an appointment to see the chief. About a story I'm doing on the casino." I dug in my backpack and pulled out my business card—the one I'd created using desktop publishing software. I'd made a bunch of different cards for every occasion.

He lifted his communication radio and said something I couldn't make out, his mouth obscured by the device. As soon he ended the call, he opened the door and let me in.

Chief Dakota Goldriver looked up from his paperwork, shuffled it together, and folded his hands on top.

Hiding something? I wondered.

"Ms. Westphal. What can I do for you?" He indicated the chair opposite him. I sat down and eyed the stack of papers, then looked up at him.

"I have something to show you," I said, pulling out copies of the photos I'd taken during my visit to the casino with my Sidekick. I spread the computer printouts on his desk. There were half a dozen, all of Bradley Edwards and the dealer he worked with. In each photo, just like in Mariposa's photos, Brad had his arms crossed. But in each snapshot, his hand shapes were different.

Dakota looked over the pictures, then up at me.

"We don't allow any kind photography in the casino. I want to protect our patrons."

"So arrest me," I said.

He frowned. "What's this about, Ms. Westphal?"

"Look at the pictures."

He glanced at them. "Yes?"

"Look at this man's hands."

Dakota lifted one of the pictures and studied it closely. He set it back down and shook his head. "And?"

"Now look at this one." I handed him another picture. He held it up and stared at it a few seconds, then set it back down.

"I'm sorry, I don't—"

"His hand shapes are different in each picture."

Dakota leaned over and peered at all six of the photos.

"Alright. And your point?"

"The man, Bradley Edwards, is signaling the dealer. He's cheating."

Dakota collected the photos in a pile and returned them to me. Not the response I was expecting.

"I know."

I sat back, smiling. "I figured you did." Now that the rat was out of the bag, would he try to kill me right here in his office? Naw, too many witnesses, although these gamblers might not care if it interfered with their chances of winning.

"I'm sorry you went to all this trouble, Ms. Westphal, but—"

"It was no trouble. As a matter of fact, I think you killed Zander Nicholas and Mariposa Sunflower because they found out about the cheating and were blackmailing you." I looked at him smugly. "And by the way, the sheriff knows I'm here."

The bastard actually grinned. "If you'd let me finish."

I nodded curtly.

"I know all about the cheating. About a week ago I discovered Edwards and Deerhunter using the sign language letters."

"Deerhunter?"

"That's his Indian name. He also goes by Lynn Morris. Anyway, I have my own photos taken with surveillance cameras hidden behind the mirrored ceiling." He pointed upward with his thumb.

I looked up, saw a reflection of myself, and wondered if I was being watched at this very moment.

"I've taken care of the problem," Dakota said.

"Really? How?"

"Edwards and Morris were fired."

My mouth dropped open. "What?"

He nodded. "Like I said, my security guards have been watching them for some time. We confronted them with the photos, they confessed, and I let them go—with the promise that we wouldn't turn them in to the sheriff if they paid back the money they had stolen from us."

"Hmm," I muttered, trying to sort out this new development. "So, you weren't in on it?"

"I'm sorry to disappoint you, Ms. Westphal, but no, I have no reason to cheat my own casino."

I stuffed my photos into my backpack and rose to leave. "One last question. Do you think Bradley might have killed Zander and Mariposa?"

He shrugged. "I have no idea. That's the sheriff's job."

I nodded. "Do you know where I can find him? Brad Edwards?"

"I have an address for him if you'd like that. But I doubt it will do you any good. I understand he's disappeared."

"Disappeared? What do you mean?"

"Just that. One of my employees went to his house and found it cleaned out, as if he'd packed up and left town suddenly."

Dakota typed something into his computer, pushed "Print," and handed the printout to me. "But here's his address if you want to check it out. Although if you do find him, I'd advise you not to go accusing him like you did me. He may not be as…reasonable as I am."

I stuffed the address in my pocket, nodded to Dakota Goldriver, and excused myself, with my tail between my legs.

As I drove along the dark gold country roads, I thought about what Dakota had said. Was he telling the truth? Would I be able to find out if he was lying? And live to tell about it?

I was so deep in thought I hadn't been paying attention to the drive, other than attempting to keep the car on the snowy road. But after a few miles, I noticed that the same headlines were still behind me. At first I'd thought nothing of it. Several people had left the casino at the same time I had.

But eventually those cars had disappeared, leaving a lone car, traveling about two to three car lengths behind me. I noticed because the driver's high beams were shining in my rearview mirror. And one was distinctly dimmer than the other. Before I went blind, I flicked the mirror to night driving mode and leaned a little so I couldn't see the lights in my side mirror.

A few miles later I came to a stop sign and checked my mirror.

The same headlights.

I strained to make out details of the car but it was dark. All I knew from the headlights was big. An SUV?

I drove on, glancing in the mirror every few seconds to see if the car was still on my tail.

Yep.

Kenny-Wayne? Trying to "pass" me again?

With one hand on the wheel, I reached into my backpack with the other, searching for my Sidekick to call for help. I located it, pulled it out, and dropped it in between the seats.

"Damn!" I said as I dug into the crack and came up empty.

Now what.

As I neared my diner home, just outside of town, I decided not to go there. I didn't want to lead this maniac—if he really was following me—to my home, where I'd be alone. I pressed on the gas pedal, passed my driveway, and turned onto Flat Skunks' Main Street.

On the edge of town, I checked the rearview mirror again.

No headlights.

I drove through town slowly, waiting for the lights to appear behind me at any second. Nothing.

Had it been my imagination? I was on edge lately after all that had happened. At the end of the short street, I made a U-turn and headed back to my diner. I had to get back home. If Dan found out I'd gone out, he'd kill me.

As I drove, I neurotically checked the mirror. My heart rate returned to normal and I petted Casper to reassure her. I checked the mirror again.

The headlights were back. High beams, one dimmer than the other.

My heart jumped to my throat.

This was not my imagination.

Enough of this crap.

I laid on the horn.

Feeling the vibration of the sound under my fingers, I spun around and stopped, facing the car head on. I switched on my brights.

A little game of chicken?

The other car stopped.

It began backing up.

Before I could start up again, the car made a wild U-turn and sped off, zigzagging down the road.

It was too dark to see the model or plate of the SUV. All I knew was someone had been following me.

For how long, I had no idea.

# 27

"Come on, Casper," I said, as I entered the car. "Let's go home before Dan finds out I left."

I patted my dog and drove home thinking about what Dakota had said. Was it true? Was he not involved in cheating at the casino? He could easily be lying.

I had to pay a visit to Bradley Edwards. But not tonight. It was too late, too dark, and I was too tired. And no way was I going to see him alone. I also made a mental note to visit Kenny-Wayne's compound and find out more about what went on out there in whackoville.

But for now, a nice hot bath while I waited for Dan to return. When I arrived at my diner, I looked around for signs of anything unusual. The place looked normal. Porch light on. Diner lit up like a casino. So far, so good.

I turned the key in the lock and entered, allowing Casper to go in first. She sniffed around but her behavior wasn't any different from usual.

"Good girl," I said, and gave her a treat. "Now let me have a soak and go over my notes, and see if I can figure out what in God's name is going on around here before someone else gets killed. Like me, for instance."

I patted her head and she followed me into the bathroom. I ran a warm bath, full of lavender scented bubbles, and settled back onto my plastic bath pillow with my notepad. All that was missing was my favorite bath toy.

I flipped open the cover and read over my notes. Dakota Goldriver was still at the top of my list. He had the most to lose if cheating at the casino was discovered—and a reason to murder Mariposa and Zander who both knew about the scheme. He appeared to be making a lot of money as CEO of the place, if that indoor gym in his office was any indication. I wondered what his home looked like. He knew Zander and India and was probably buying pot from them. He was powerful enough to strangle Zander and Mariposa. The kicker was he might not even be Indian. But he denied anything to do with cheating and had blamed Bradley Edwards and some guy named Morris. If Dakota was involved too, wouldn't he be worried that Brad would expose him?

Dakota had said that Bradley had disappeared after being fired.

Disappeared like India? And possibly murdered like India?

Whoa, Connor. Take it down a notch. There were other suspects to consider. Such as Kenny-Wayne Johnson. He was probably capable of killing—he seemed to prepare for it daily with all his para-military gear and propaganda. He was a little nuts from smoking all that dope—he practically ran me off the road just trying to pass me. He certainly had the muscle to strangle two people. And he knew Zander and India. Maybe Mariposa was blackmailing him too—for what reason, I wasn't sure. But I sensed it had to do with his plans to overthrow the government, if he didn't shoot himself in the foot first.

Bradley Edwards, who had been third on my list, was a strange one. Not terrible friendly, although that didn't make him a murderer necessarily. But he was involved in cheating at the casino, which was making him enough money to buy a town. The sign that last left at my diner home after the intrusion was a giveaway. It had read *Deafie*. Not a lot of hearing people know the term that Deaf people used among themselves. He, too, was strong enough to strangle a couple of people. And if Mariposa was blackmailing him, he had motive.

But where was he now?

The Carters were a long shot. They were big, true, but big didn't always mean powerful. And if they had a reason, I hadn't discovered it yet. Little-Ruth had mentioned that Mariposa was out at their place snooping around and taking pictures. More blackmail? Very possible. But I couldn't see the church ladies climbing up trees and onto rooftops. Maybe they had someone working for them?

As for opportunity, hell, all the suspects would have had plenty of time and opportunity to murder Zander and Mariposa.

And now India. I had a feeling the worst had happened. All that blood. Her dogs trapped in the basement. The fire. And she'd indicated she was afraid for her life. She probably had access to Zander's computer and knew all about the blackmail business. At this point it appeared as if the killer was trying to eliminate anyone associated with the crime.

Including me.

Did I know something and not know it?

My mind kept going back to the rope. The rope around Zander's neck, Mariposa's neck, Casper's neck.

What was it about the rope that bothered me?

I started doodling words, free associating, even trying to channel answers from the great beyond.

Rope. Hemp. India.
India. Zander. Dealing.
Dealing. Casino. Dakota.
Dakota. Token. Cheating.
Cheating. Bradley. Deaf.
Deaf. Josh. Land.
Land. Environment. Tree.
Tree. Mariposa. Flower.
Flower. Bud. Marijuana.
Marijuana. Hallucinogen. Religion.
Religion. Carters. Wealth.
Wealth. Dealing. Pot.
Pot. Hemp. Rope.
Rope. Dope. Soap.

Soap. Time to scrub up and get out before I turned into a—
Casper's head began snapping. What was she barking at now?

I looked over.

"What is it, Casper?"

Casper sprinted out of the bathroom.

Something was up.

I put my notepad down, stood up, and grabbed a towel. Wrapping it around me, I stepped out and headed for the living area. I could see Casper's tail wagging at the front door.

Was someone there?

I looked at my door light. Odd. It wasn't flashing. Maybe the visitor didn't know I was deaf and had knocked instead of ringing the bell.

If that was the case, I wasn't about to answer.

Casper's head snapped wildly. Whoever it was would know that Casper was inside. Surely they could hear the barking.

I inched up to the door and peered through the peephole. The porch light was off. I must have switched it off. If I switched it back on, they would know I was home. But without it I couldn't see who it was.

I moved to the front window of the diner and peeked through the blinds. A large dark SUV sat in my driveway. It was hard to make out the model and plate.

I had no choice. I returned to the front door, switched on the porch light, and peeked again through the peephole. I was glad I did.

"Oh my God!"

I undid the three locks as quickly as I could and jerked open the door.

India stood on my front porch.

Covered in blood.

# 28

"India!" I eased her inside, relocked the door, and led her to a seat in my diner kitchen. She looked like she'd lost a lot of blood, judging by the amount smeared on her face, arms, and hand. The other hand was bound with a bloody towel. I threw on a robe and grabbed some fresh towels and Bactine. After cleaning up the blood, I re-bandaged a cut on her wrist, which seemed to be the source of the bleeding. I couldn't find any other cuts or stab wounds.

She'd been lucky.

When I finished, I got her a cup of tea—cranberry, no hemp. While she sipped it, I picked up the TDD phone.

India, her eyes wide with fear, nearly dropped her teacup as she bolted from her seat. She grabbed the receiver out of my hand and slammed it down. "What are you doing?"

"I'm...I was just calling an ambulance. You need to see a doctor." I was startled by her sudden strength. Her adrenaline must have been what kept her alive during that knife attack.

"No! No doctor. No sheriff. No one. He's after me, don't you understand?"

Stunned at her overreaction, I eased her back to her seat and handed her the teacup. "It's all right, India. You're safe here. The house is locked tight. Dan will be back soon. But you really need to get medical treatment for that wrist cut."

She shook her head and rubbed at the tears in her eyes.

I placed my hand on her knee. "Can you tell me what happened?"

She set the cup down and looked away, as if reliving the event. "He...he had a knife...he tried to...to kill me—"

"Who, India? Who tried to kill you?"

"He was looking for...photos..."

Dakota.

"India, was it Dakota Goldriver?"

Her eyes widened as her gaze shifted to something behind me.

I spun around.

"Casper!" My dog stood in the doorway, her teeth bared, her head down.

"Casper! Stop!" I commanded.

She scratched at something at her feet. Something she had apparently brought in and dropped.

A rope.

"What, Casper? What is it?"

I picked it up. It was the rope Dan had found around Casper's neck. Odd. I thought I'd disposed of it. I ran my fingers over the textured, rough surface. Hemp. I was becoming an expert at recognizing the stuff.

I turned to India and held it up, confused. "Is this—"

The color had drained from India's face. She looked as if she'd seen a ghost.

"Are you all right?"

India leapt from her seat and snatched the rope from my hand.

"India—"

I looked at her. And knew.

Casper was barking because she recognized India.

India was the one who'd put that rope around Casper's neck.

I reached for my Sidekick but I was too late. In a blur of movement, India shoved me to the floor and planting a knee on my back, threw the loop over my head. She tightened it around my neck.

"Cas—" I tried to speak but choked on the words. Grabbing the rope at my neck, I tried to my fingers underneath it.

India was incredibly strong. The rope tightened. My neck and face throbbed painfully.

I gasped for air.

I swung my arms wildly trying to knock her off balance. She was just out of reach. I kicked backwards. She jumped away, still holding the rope tight.

Tighter.

*Casper!* In the corner of my eye I saw my dog jumping and snapping at India.

*Help me, Casper!*

India's grip held firm. I started to see patches of darkness.

I made a last ditch attempt to free myself. Instead of fighting against her, I arched backward, the direction of her pull. The back of my head smacked her square in the chest.

India lost her balance and fell back, releasing the rope in the process. I tried to roll away, but she grabbed me around the waist and pulled me back.

I swung my arms, trying to bash her senseless, but she held firm. I looked around for something to hit her with and spotted the tree-climbing gadget that had been used on Dan.

Just out of reach.

"Casper! Fetch!" I signed and pointed.

India punched me in the side and I doubled over.

Casper barked.

I repeated the command, a little less enthusiastically.

Casper stopped barking and looked in the direction I'd pointed to.

She pounced.

And brought back one of my Uggs.

"No, Casper! Fetch!" I pointed again.

India tightened her grip on me and moved a hand to my neck. She began squeezing. Even one-handed, India was strong.

Casper pounced again.

This time she brought back the weapon India had used on Dan.

India reached for it but I beat her to it.

Grasping it in my hand, I slammed it against India's arm. And then I hit her again on the shoulder. And then her temple.

She released her grip and melted to the floor.

Quickly, I rolled over and stood up, rubbing my neck and gasping for air.

India was only capable of rolling her eyes. Casper snarled at her, zigzagging from side to side. I knew Casper would never bite anyone, but India didn't know that. She was used to dogs that bit anything that moved.

I bent down and grasped Casper's collar. To India I said, "You move one inch and I'll release her. She'll tear you apart." I wasn't sure she heard me at that point, but it felt good to say.

Casper bared her teeth and lowered her head. This dog could have her own TV show, she was such a good actress.

I snatched the rope from India and used it to bind her hands and legs. In double knots. Tight. Then I added some twine of my own. By the time I was finished tying her up, she looked like one of her macramé creations.

As I leaned over to retrieve my Sidekick that had fallen out of my pocket during the scuffle, I noticed a shiny object on the floor next to India's foot.

I picked it up. A token. From the Gold Strike Casino.

I turned on the Sidekick, punched in Dan's email, and sent him an instant message. It read: "Cm Quick. Everything all tied up..."

# 29

After the crowd cleared out and India was carted off to jail in Bogus Thunder, Dan and I snuggled into my sofa bed with bowls of Quarterback Crunch ice cream and a couple of Tylenol to review the events. I jotted occasional notes to use for my headline story, planning to be at the office at the crack of dawn.

"So I was right about Zander and India selling large amounts of pot to lots of people."

Dan nodded and took a spoonful of ice cream. "Dakota bought it from him to use as bonuses for his workers. Kenny-Wayne used it to entice misfits into joining his survivalist clan. The Carters bought and sold it to church members to fund their extravagant ministry. And Mariposa got it for free, so to speak."

"You found all that out from Zander's computer files?"

"Yep. He also had a secret file that India may have discovered. It was filled with love letters written to Mariposa. Despite their age difference, he was really smitten. Looks like he planned to sell his assets, leave India, and go off with the girl."

"And that was the real reason India killed him. And Mariposa. She was jealous. Both murders...they had nothing to do with the pot farm, did they?"

"Not really, although the pot farm funded their real estate ventures. They'd bought up all kinds of land in the gold country. Land that will no doubt be golden in a few years thanks to the influx of retirees, burned-out Yuppies, radical groups, and all that comes with them."

"And that's why they didn't appear to have much in the way of material goods. It all went into the purchase of land. Dakota knew a gold mine when he saw one."

I fed Dan a spoonful of my ice cream, a true sign of commitment. I don't part easily with my Quarterback Crunch.

"But how did India get Zander up on the roof in order to hang him? She's strong," I rubbed my neck, remembering her force, "but not that strong."

"Well, he was loaded, so to speak. I figure she told him there was something he needed to see from there, like the pot farm. Unlikely, but when you're paranoid, you worry about everything."

"Or maybe she sent him a forged note from Mariposa, asking to meet him up there," I added.

"Maybe. We may never know. But by the time he got there, he was pretty doped up. India planned it well. The dummy had already been removed. All she had to do was get that rope around him and push him off the roof. In his drugged state, that wouldn't have been too hard."

"Without anyone seeing them?"

"It was the middle of the night. This town is dead after the bars close."

"Poor choice of words." I scraped the bottom of the ice cream bowl. "And the coin?"

"I haven't quite figured that out. She must have stuck it between his fingers somehow, with a little glue. Maybe after he died. Would have been easier just to stick it in his pocket. But she really wanted to make a point."

"That Dakota Goldriver murdered him. Which he didn't." I eyed Dan's bowl of ice cream. He still had some left.

"Right. She tried to make it look like Dakota did it when she found out about the cheating at the casino. India was angry at the tribe because they owned land that India and Zander wanted as part of their real estate investment."

"And what about the cheating?" I asked.

"Sheriff is looking into it. He found copies of Mariposa's photos on Zander's computer. Dakota denies knowing anything, and I think he's telling the truth. But Bradley Edwards and one of the dealers are being investigated. They were using sign language, no less."

"What about the church ladies? Did they have anything to do with their pastor's death?"

"No way of telling, unfortunately. The case is too old. But the IRS is looking into their 'tax-free' status."

"And Kenny-Wayne?"

"He'll probably be arrested for stupidity."

I laughed, then thought a minute as I licked my spoon clean. What about Josh? What would become of his DeafTown now that Bradley was under investigation? I thought of little Susie. My heart ached for her. No mother. A dreamer for a father. And now practically homeless.

Dan interrupted my thoughts. "All this for land," he mused.

I nodded. "In spite of being potheads, India and Zander were smarter than I thought."

"Well, India got caught. She wasn't that smart," Dan said, handing me his bowl. "And Zander got killed."

I helped myself to a spoonful. "So, India cut her hand to make it look like Dakota stabbed her with her kitchen knife. No wonder she was so strong. She really hadn't lost much blood. She must made it look like that."

"Right. When she caught you snooping, and she tied you up in her hidden room, and after removing all her valuable paperwork and the blackmail photos she stole from Mariposa, she set fire to the place, and the pot farm, to cover her tracks and make it look like someone was after her. She figured the sheriff would believe she was dead, even without a body." Dan wiped a drip of ice cream from my cheek and licked his finger.

"Then she'd sell off all her property, take the money, and start over somewhere else." I thought for a moment. "So she's the one who hit you over the head with that climbing gizmo?"

Dan shrugged. "I suppose. She must have stolen it from Mariposa to incriminate her too."

"And she wrote 'Deafie' on that sign she left next to Casper, after wrapping that rope around her neck. Where did she learn that term?"

"Probably from Bradley. Remember, he was a regular customer of hers and Zander's."

"Wait a minute. How did she get Mariposa up on that overhang?" I asked. "Think she was taking steroids, in addition to all that weed?"

Dan laughed. "She could have hoisted her up there with the rope, after strangling her. With all those branches, she could have made some kind of pulley. And obviously she removed the ladder, hoping to scare you off."

I shook my head. "Wow. She was amazing."

"Speaking of amazing," Dan said, "how did you get those dogs to obey you?"

"I'm not exactly sure. I tried doggy treats but they inhaled them. I remembered India giving them a command at the door. When I read her lips, it looked like she said, 'pa-lay' or 'ba-lay.' I have no idea what the real word was, but I must have come close."

Dan thought for moment. I watched his lips as he said something that looked like, "Par-aye?"

"Looks the same. What does it mean?"

"*P-a-r-e*. It's Spanish for 'stop!'"

"So now I can lip-read in Spanish!"

I got up, walked over to a shelf that held stacks of my comic books, cartoon action figures, and box games. Grabbing a deck of Looney Tunes-backed cards, I brought them over to the sofa bed and began shuffling.

"What are you doing?" Dan asked, grinning.

"I'm going to teach you a new game."

"That's funny. I was going to teach you a new game tonight too. But it doesn't involve cards."

I smiled. "This game is almost as fun. I got it off the Internet. If I win, you have to remove an article of clothing and play again. If I lose, we can play your game."

Dan looked down at himself. "Connor, I'm only wearing pajama bottoms."

I smiled again. "I know."

"So what's the game? Strip Poker? Strip Old Maid? Strip Solitaire?"

I looked at him. "It's called Dead Man's Hand—"

My door light suddenly flashed on and off. I looked at Dan and then the clock on the wall.

"Kind of late. Expecting someone?" he asked.

I shook my head. "No, I've had enough company tonight. You?"

"Nope. Could be the sheriff. Maybe he's found out something else."

As I slipped on my robe, Dan signed, "Peephole, remember."

I smiled. "Didn't do me much good when India was at the door, did it? She didn't need to break in. I let her waltz right in so she could try to murder me."

I headed for the door.

Peering through the peephole, I recognized the figure in the porch light. Reluctantly I unfastened the locks and opened the door halfway.

"Hi Josh," I signed without using my voice. "What are you doing here so late?" I looked at my watch for emphasis. "Where's Susie?"

"Hey, Con. She's asleep in the car." He glanced back at the SUV. "We just got back from visiting Brad in jail. You were right..."

I shook my head. "It's late, Josh. And I'm tired."

"I know, I know, but I asked you a question earlier. Could I come by tomorrow so we can talk?"

I brought my hands together and felt my ring. I removed it from my right hand, and slid it onto my left hand.

"I'm sorry, Josh, I..." I held my left hand up.

Josh saw the ring, nodded, and lowered his head. "Dan?"

I nodded.

He took my left hand in his and kissed it. "He's a lucky guy," he signed.

Then he turned and headed for his car.

I closed the door and stood in the entryway, staring at the gold nugget ring which now sparkled on my left hand.

Dan was sitting up waiting for me when I returned.

I sat next to him and took his right hand with my left hand. "You know, Dan, after all the chances I've taken with my life, it's about time I took a chance on marriage, don't you think?"

Dan's mouth dropped open. "Really?" he signed, pushing his index finger up his chin.

I nodded.

"When?" he signed.

"How about as soon as the snow thaws? I really don't want to wear Uggs and a parka on my wedding day."

Dan looked at the ring on my left hand.

For the first time, I saw tears in Dan's eyes.

Penny Warner has published over 40 books, including seven mysteries in the award-winning Connor Westphal series. DEAD BODY LANGUAGE was nominated for an Agatha Award and won a Macavity Award for Best First Mystery. The series has been optioned by Andrea Farrell from "7th Heaven" and Marlee Matlin, award winning actress from "Children of a Lesser God." Warner also writes a series for middle-grade readers, featuring a scout troop that solves mysteries involving historic, environmental and social issues. MYSTERY OF THE HAUNTED CAVES won an Agatha Award and an Anthony Award for Best Juvenile Mystery. Her books have been published internationally, in over a dozen languages.

Warner has a Bachelor's Degree in Child Development and Master's Degree in Special Education with a focus on Deaf Education and American Sign Language. She teaches at the local college and leads mystery writing courses at California State University Hayward, UC Berkeley, Book Passage, and M is for Mystery. She has spoken at numerous writing conferences, including Bouchercon World Mystery, Left Coast Crime, Sleuthfest, Cluefest, Malice Domestic, Cuesta College, Harriette Austin, Pikes Peak, San Francisco Writers, Jack London, East of Eden, William Saroyan, Sisters in Crime, Mystery Writers of America, and California Writers Club conferences. She has appeared on television promoting her books, written a weekly newspaper column, and currently writes for several websites. With her husband Tom, she writes and produces murder mystery events for libraries and other organizations across the country. Warner lives in Danville with her husband and has two children.